The
Well of
Saint
Nobody

Neil Jordan

The Well of Saint Nobody

An Apollo Book

First published in the UK in 2023 by Head of Zeus Ltd,
part of Bloomsbury Publishing Plc.

9 7 5 3 1 2 4 6 8

A catalogue record for this book is available from the British Library.

ISBN (HB): 9781804549810
ISBN (XTPB): 9781035902989
ISBN (E): 9781804549797

Typeset by Divaddict Publishing Solutions

Printed and bound in Great Britain by
CPI Group (UK) Ltd, Croydon CR0 4YY

Head of Zeus Ltd
5–8 Hardwick Street
London EC1R 4RG

WWW.HEADOFZEUS.COM

For Caoimhe, Faye and Max.

PART ONE

1

He had met her three times and three times forgotten all about her.

As if meeting a different person, and there had to be, she eventually came to realize, a kind of truth in that.

The first time was in what was then called the Francis Xavier, a run-down concert hall round about where Drumcondra Road crossed the canal and turned into Dorset Street. It housed the RTE symphony orchestra, which was always at that time in search of a premises, but proved a suitable venue for the instrumental section of the Father Matthew Feis Ceoil. A competition involving student violinists, cellists, pianists and classical guitarists (a quite recent innovation, but it was the seventies, after all).

She was a pianist, as was he. She was fifteen, he was in his late twenties, in the full flush of an international career that would only much, much later come to a shuddering and chaotic halt. He was the international adjudicator, flown over from London, a rather thin, tall and indefinably distracted figure, not totally unaware of the hint of glamour he brought to the drab proceedings. She hardly dared look at him when she walked on the stage, but she had seen his face and profile on album covers, the Rachmaninoff one her favourite, the lock of hair

3

tumbling over his elegant forehead towards the piano keys, so she probably had no need to. She caught a glimpse of that profile as she bowed to the distant adjudicators below, sheet music in one hand, and she could imagine it as she ploughed her way through the preludes and fugues of *The Well-Tempered Clavier*. She couldn't have played more than two of them and, years later, couldn't remember which ones she played. Though she remembered everything else. The sunlight pouring through the high churchlike windows, the squeak of the pedal, which she always used too much of, the sweat, flowing from her hands to the already sweaty piano keys. There had been others before her, and there would be one other after. She would remember the effortless mastery of that other, who would go on to win the prize. Such a level of dexterity and excellence, she would remember thinking, would always be beyond her. And her hands, as he mentioned, when the laurels were eventually handed out, were on the small side. He shook them, and she evaded his glance, took the rolled diploma with its special mention, shook hands with the other adjudicators and walked down that hall, trying to hold back the tears. Why she was crying she wasn't sure. An honourable mention wasn't that bad. But she would remember the scent of aftershave when she listened back to his recording of the Rachmaninoff, which she now knew she would never master. It must have been his.

So to see him again, in the small West Cork village, in the windy end of March, at a table outside the coffee shop, one crabbed hand bent around a herbal tea, was quite a shock. The other hand was removing an untidy face mask, to enable him to bring the cup to his lips. So she could see that profile again, above the untidy clump of the blue face covering, tucked like a scarf around his chin. The hair that tumbled down the creased forehead was grey now. She had heard someone had bought the old archbishop's house, a musician of some kind, and had a mental image of some long-haired rock and roll guitarist still clinging to the sartorial style of the late seventies, with a leather pea coat, stacked heels and a pair of dark glasses to disguise those eyes that nobody would have recognized anyway.

But nothing could have prepared her for the sight of him, wrapped in a scarf and a parka, the cuffs of his trousers riding too high, revealing unmatching socks and a pair of trainers that any teenager (or pensioner) might wear, looking windswept, irritable and unmistakably old.

He somehow belonged there, the way she belonged. The way the other random arrivals could never belong, winter inhabitants of summer cottages, blown down here by the wind of the latter end of the pandemic.

She examined her own hands as she passed him. Still on the small side, she thought, hardly able to stretch over an octave, from little finger to thumb. Still, they were well preserved, which were more than she could say for his. Covered in blisters, she noted, and redly peeling skin, the long fingers stretching easily round the earthenware teacup. What she wouldn't have done for such long fingers, aged fifteen, when she first saw him and in her later conservatory days.

And they say hand-span doesn't matter. She made her way past, with a gust of following wind, and would have sensed his glance, had he raised his head to notice her passing. But she suspected he wouldn't. And maybe it was better, she thought to herself, to remain unnoticed and unremembered.

But he noticed something, of course he did. He was used to perusal, the kind of generic attention to the approach, the departure, the presence of a woman. The sound of heels on a pavement. The presence of a scent, somewhere outside his vision. A rippling laugh, a voice on a mobile phone. Signals that alerted him to the bother of raising his head and looking. But she had cork-sandalled soles and hadn't worn perfume for a long time. Her mobile phone was at home, on the kitchen table. So he knew a woman had passed him, but didn't take the trouble to look.

His hands. The crusted flakes of skin around the knuckles, the reddened sores, the weeping pustules. His throat ached for a coffee, but he had given up dairy and so he waited for whatever tannic kick the herbal tea might provide. But there was none. A whiff of steam up his nostrils, the taste of sloe berries, like a non-alcoholic gin. So that was it, he thought, for a while at least.

He finished the tea and rose, went back inside the shop to pay. He pulled the face mask back up before he entered. Mary, buxom behind her patterned apron, watched him approach. Through the window, obscured by the thin dapple of mist, then through the open doorway, walking with the mildest stoop for a man of his age, rustling for coins in his left-hand pocket.

She had heard of him, of course. And with that strange deflected grace of the Irish countryside, pretended she hadn't. He was famous for something or other. Not the bass guitar, like that long-haired streel down by Clonakilty who used to play with Jimi Hendrix. No, it was the piano.

"How much, my dear?" he asked. She looked at his crabbed hand on the butcher's block counter and wondered was this endearment a tease or a presumption.

"Two fifty," she said. She almost added an ironic "sir". But she held her tongue, deciding it was neither. He was a man used, too used, to easy familiarity. Others were always an audience for him. A sea of faces, no need to distinguish one from the other.

"If I could ask a small favour," he began, and took a piece of folded paper from the pocket of his parka.

"Whatever we can do to help, sir." The sir came out of her mouth unbidden, with no irony attached, and he hardly seemed to register it. And any hint of amusement would be hidden by the cloth that covered her mouth. She wondered did her eyes give away the smile, above it.

"That noticeboard, by the fridge—"

"The freezer, sir."

"Of course. The freezer."

"Could I place a small announcement there?"

"Of course. Whatever you want."

"And is there a charge?"

"For a few words, stuck to the boards? No. No charge at all, sir."

"And you don't have to call me sir. I haven't been knighted."

Mary smiled.

"Not yet, sir."

"Though we live in hope. But until that happy day, the name is William."

William. So that was his name, she thought. William something or other. He had played at the Bantry House Festival, she had been told. Though she couldn't help wondering what those damaged hands could play now, as they plucked a pin from the cork noticeboard and affixed a folded page, filled out with neat cursive.

"Be our guest, William."

"Thank you, my dear."

And he left, not bothering to read the plastic name-tag attached to her bosomy apron, which read Mary Culleton. And Mary Culleton could read from here the message attached to the noticeboard by the freezer.

Wanted.
Housekeeper.
Possible Cooking Duties.
Please Contact:
The Rectory
Old Bawn
Orran
Co. Cork.

Mary kept an eye on his exit. She found herself amused by the pedantry of the notice. Who didn't know that Orran was a village in West Cork? A foreigner, maybe. An asylum seeker, from one of those run-down hotels on the Bantry Road. The wind flapped his khaki jacket at the doorway and made two rippling flags of the trousers round his ankles. She glimpsed the garish mismatched socks and the trainers below them before he moved behind the patina of the misted window. There was a term for whatever style that was. Eccentric. Past it. Relic of old decency.

And out he walked. Down the curving main street, past the SuperValu and the three pubs that still plied their trade. His heels chafed. His knees creaked. He could have driven but forced himself to walk. A bicycle could become an option when he gathered the energy to buy himself one.

He had first seen the village in summer, crowded for the Bantry House music festival. It had seemed innocent, out of the way and somehow out of time, with the wind pulling flecks of white from the ocean and skinny kids diving in from the pier. He had let it drop to Susannah that a great-grandmother or a great-aunt came from somewhere not too far from here. They had driven then, further and further afield, until they finally tracked down a gravestone, almost in an adjacent county. "From here" to him meant Cork, Ireland, a remembered attachment that simply buttressed his essential Englishness. He would find that "from here" to the locals meant something quite different. His aunt had left long before the War of Independence, so the attachment was to a broader, more tranquil sense of empire. He played Ravel's *Gaspard de la Nuit* and Bartok's *2nd Concerto* in Bantry House and leavened their severity with some of the Field Nocturnes, and was quite overwhelmed by the audience response. Any nod to Irishness, he was to find, elicited something like this. So the thought of his own tenuous thread to this place filled him with warmth, as did the possibility of another life, and another past that could have been. They had seen the empty rectory from the road and arranged a viewing. One of the few that had not been burnt in those faraway troubles, it had an elegance and a seductive emptiness that seemed to be begging for restoration. They had entertained the thought they might someday live there, in the first flush of their attempted union. That flush was to fade of course, into pallid tones of blame and uninterest, but the memory of the rectory stayed with him, and when Jeremy Morton, late of BBC Four, mentioned it had come up for sale again, he found himself, almost without any agency of his own, like a sleepwalker, buying it, without any second viewing. Jeremy had restored a farmhouse by the estuary. Pastoral retirement, in a place half remembered by a forgotten great-aunt. A home for a love that never quite happened. There was an irony there, he thought, as he walked. And irony was one of the few pleasures left to him.

Past the breeze-block school, with the basketball hoop in the front courtyard. The church, with the graveyard sloping up the hill behind it. It took about forty minutes to reach his own rusted gates. Beyond them, the avenue, lined irregularly by elm and poplar trees. In France they would have been immaculate, groomed, symmetrical. Here they were like random, accidentally vertical extensions of the hedgerow. The slow rise of the ocean behind them, flecked by a white horse's mane of foam. The wind dictated everything here. It stripped the trees bare, made his trousers flap, drove the mist horizontal. It gathered mounds of leaves around the rectory gates, made the gates themselves creak, in grinding, repeating semitones. And now he pushed the gate fully open, made his way up the gravelled path.

The old Jaguar sat in the forecourt. It had waited there, patient and inert, for a full week now. He didn't feel like driving. He didn't feel much at all, apart from waiting out the end of this confinement, in this house he had only lately taken the trouble to inhabit. He reminded himself once more to cut back those rhododendrons. They were threatening to overwhelm what the estate agent had grandly termed the orchard. With a chainsaw, if his hands could manage it. With a hired gardener, if they couldn't. He himself drew the key from his pocket and inserted it in the rectory door. And as the door creaked open, he had to remind himself once again how much he had hoped to love this place.

On days like this it took some reminding. The grand piano sat in a rectangle of pale light coming through the curved bay window. Through it he could see the slow rise and fall of the waters of the bay beyond, like an undulating curtain of dove-grey silk. The distant boom of the wind echoed through the house and a flurry of leaves the opening door allowed in drifted around the packing cases.

A film of dust was gathering on them. His books, manuscripts, albums, awards, dress-suits, the case of the cello which he had promised to take up again. He had unpacked what he called his day-clothes, two speakers which had been inexpertly cabled to the plug outlets in the crumbling walls.

But the piano was the real evidence that the house was, or was intended to be, lived in. It sat there, like an old lover waiting for attention. The lid was up and so the same dust that gathered on the packing cases was now gathering on the keys. It had been three weeks since he had tried to uncrunch his fingers and make the familiar sounds on them. He used the thumb of his left hand now in yet one more attempt to flex the fingers of his right. He could hear the soft cracks they emitted and feel the itching, the scraped stretching of the skin. Well then, he thought, if he couldn't play, he could try to write. He could maybe even peel an onion, crack an egg and cook.

2

Tara had walked past, ducked inside the SuperValu, and was not pretending to peruse the array of health food products beneath the long plate-glass window. No, she genuinely needed some of those seaweed flakes and the antioxidants and iron supplements and those blueberries that were advertised as Irish but most likely came from Morocco or Peru. But she was afforded a glimpse from there of the domed forehead with its flap of greying hair blowing in the wind as he made his way past. The whole street outside was her little cinema and his was the only walk-on part. She wondered how she herself must look, after a gap of twenty or more years. She wondered was that the curse that his kind of fame brought with it. To be always contrasted with the image of your younger self. Who could remember what she looked like, aged fifteen, playing her Bach fugues under his disinterested gaze? Definitely not him. She was in her post-punk phase when she met him six years later, in the green room of the Wigmore Hall, told him how thrilling it was to hear his Hayden's 11th in person, so daringly paired with Ravel's *Concerto for the Left Hand*. He had stretched and unstretched the long, elegant fingers of his own left hand and talked abstractedly about the darkness of the piece. An accidental consequence of the muting of the right. Or of Wittgenstein, his pianist brother, the trenches of the First World War. Then he had stretched the same left hand to accept a glass of champagne, and turned away, with perfect manners, and once more forgotten her completely. There would be a third time, in Brighton, and the less said about that the better, maybe.

Or maybe not, she mused, as his profile glided down the windy street and out of sight. We are all famous to ourselves. And those who have never known fame know what it is to be forgotten.

She bought a punnet of blueberries and a sachet of dried seaweed and made her way back to the house. It was beyond a small stretch of two-up, two-downs on a street that curved away from the main that once had a view of the harbour. Now a semi-circle of holiday rentals denied her that pleasure. Her own cottage was hidden behind this arrangement, in a lane with a dry stone wall that backed onto a wilderness of trees, with the white-flecked ocean visible barely between them. She missed knowing what the weather would be like from her first view of the harbour in the morning. But she felt it on her face most days, the cut of the wind or the balm of the mist, and regarded her bones as weather vane. Her bones and her skin. The stiffness of the first, the drought of the second. The wind hit her face now, as she turned off Main Street, and she pictured the clothes she'd hung, flapping in it. My mother and your mother were hanging out their clothes. My mother gave your mother a punch in the nose.

She saw, with some relief, that there was no white HiAce van parked outside her gate. Having given Peter the boot two months ago, his intermittent returns "to pick up some things" always made her palms sweat. Every two days during the first month, once a week during the second – maybe they had, and the pun made her smile inwardly, petered out. She wondered was she suffering from some post-traumatic stress thing. He had never gotten physical, but a mood can make the teeth clench as much as a slap.

But he could always have parked somewhere else and walked. She pushed open the gate and looked for traces of the mud of those builder's boots of his on the dirty concrete. She didn't find them, but still turned the key gently in the lock, pushed the door open with hardly a creak.

"Peter?" she called and the cat tripped down the stairs to nudge her.

The bird squawked.

The wind thumped against the bay window.

There was nobody there.

And her relief, as she leaned back against the door, closing it behind, surprised her. Had it really been that bad? The crop of reddish hair with the balding pate sleeping in the bed beside her. The thick builder's hands, rough with her body, but able to subdue the garden at least, keep the house in some order. Maybe the Internet was right. It was all an imposition, a mild version of rape, something, what was the word, non-consensual in its very essence. But one thing was certain. She didn't miss him now.

She heard the parrot whistle the first few bars of Satie's *Gnossienne No. 1*. She had begun whistling "Moon River" to him as a joke. She couldn't be certain, but had always assumed it was male. But she then found it repeated back to her with far too much enthusiasm, and in a veritable blur of half tones. So she tried him with the Satie, assuming the simple melody and broader intervals might be a help. Bam bam ba bam bam ba bam bam baaaa. And now it had become Erik's signature tune. She whistled it back, and called his name and heard her name repeated. And maybe, she thought, he was all the company she needed. Maybe someday he'd whistle the *Goldberg Variations*.

She had enquired about a companion bird for him, and was told by the pet-shop owner that without careful introduction, supervision and a lot of luck two Amazon Greens might tear each other to shreds. A little like humans, she had muttered, eliciting a laugh.

She walked through to the kitchen and half-unpeeled a banana, took one slow bite and squeezed the rest, peel and all, through the bars of the cage. She was doing her best not to think about that which soon must be thought about. Erik's lizard eye gazed at her bleakly. She didn't mind. She knew he needed her. And even if he were to love her, his eye couldn't show it. Its Mesolithic, basilisk and pitiless stare would be the same, were she alive or dead. Then the doorbell rang and she remembered her twelve o'clock.

It was Brian, with his unlovely face under a mess of windblown curls and his manuscript book in his pudgy hand.

"Hello, Brian," she said and stepped aside to allow him in. He had forgotten his mask, of course, so she had to hand him one. She reminded herself to wash the piano keys after their lesson. A patina of jam, or maybe sugary honey, always clung to the ones he had fingered. And it would spread, if she forgot about it, to every key within her reach.

"Here," she mumbled and took a tea towel from the kitchen table, and wiped his fingers with it. Though it would do little good. He was chewing some kind of gum or toffee beneath the mask that she knew would spread through some strange osmosis to the ivories. Dribbling, possibly, since he hummed, open mouthed, as he played.

His mother loved him, she presumed. She found it hard to imagine how, as he worked through his latest assault on *Für Elise*.

★

She was back in Culleton's by ten past one. She ordered a quiche and a coffee, and as she filled a plate with salad, she noticed the elegant, old-fashioned writing, pinned to the cork noticeboard.

Wanted.
Housekeeper.
Possible cooking duties.

It was written on old rectory printed notepaper, so the handwritten address was hardly needed. And she was wondering idly about such repetition when Mary's voice interrupted.

"You interested?"

"Are you taking the piss, Mary?"

"Well, come on. How many lessons do you have a week?"

"Enough to save me from 'possible cooking duties'."

"You'd be in good company, anyways."

"Would I?"

"The best. You want to hear his voice, like one of those gents you see on the telly. Dirk Bogarde. Like velvet."

"You mean he speaks the Queen's English?"

"And a piano player, I've been told. Like yourself."

"Maybe he'd give me a lesson or two."

"So you are interested?"

"You know what, Mary?"

The doorbell chimed, as someone entered.

"What?"

"If I was I wouldn't tell you."

She became aware of her voice suddenly, as Mary attended to the newcomer. She went outside to enjoy her coffee and her quiche. That West Cork sing-song. How long since she'd acquired it? What had started as a kind of humorous imitation had somehow, lately, become her accent. What an odd journey her voice must have made. From Northside middle-class Dublin, through those years in London, stopovers in France, San Francisco and now for this West Cork backwater to become the cushion to her middle years. Would she die here? To be commemorated in the same curving tones? Every statement a question, ending on a higher lilt?

"Didn't her mother come from here?"

"Why wouldn't we welcome her?"

"Almost like a local."

"Didn't she teach half the kids in the parish?"

The parish. What on earth was the parish? She was imagining her own funeral, behind the stark piece of sixties modernism that was the parish church. She would have preferred the Protestant graveyard adjacent to her cottage, the forgotten stone frontage and the yew trees behind it. But here she was, internalizing her own demise, she realized. Sitting where he had sat. Something was wrong. She chewed her salad and gathered the last crumbs of the quiche from her plate on her fork. She had never been lonely here. The place had cured her of that crippling isolation that once plagued her in cities. But the last builder to tousle her bedclothes had gone. If she was a plant, she would be a weeping willow by a dried-up riverbank. She was an ageing piano teacher, with barely enough pupils to pay the month's rent. And that was when she knew she would finish her coffee, take her bike and make the long slow climb towards the rectory gates.

3

He was arranging papers on the tops of two packing cases when she was pushing open the gates. A page fluttered from an old binder and he was bending to pick it up – an action that would have flowed in one simple movement some years ago, but now took several, as if his spine was a rusted compass – when he saw the red flash of some movement down the avenue. The glass in the bay window was bubbled. A feature that had attracted him to the property in the first place. Georgian – or was it early Victorian? – in its authenticity. So what he saw was a globule of red, which could well have been a drop of blood, behind the pencil-like lines which he knew signified the rectory gates.

Someone was coming. The postman never wore red and besides, it was approaching mid-afternoon. So he stood, as rapidly as his rusted spine would permit, the errant paper between his flaking fingers. He surprised himself then by a flutter of anticipation. He saw the gates open, soundlessly, though he could imagine their grinding creak filling the ears of whoever it was that was pushing. A woman, he gathered, as his eyes now distinguished a red raincoat, flaring down to the knees. There was a bicycle, held in one hand, the other hand pushing open the right-hand gate, which was closed again, dutifully, as the red raincoat leaned back against it.

The postman would have left it open, he thought idly, watching the duo move up the avenue, raincoat and bike, walking, not cycling. The elm and the poplar trees threw shadows across the bike's path and the leaves blew in clusters and he felt that flutter of anticipation again. Company.

Someone was coming, to break the isolation of the afternoon. There would be conversation, a message delivered, pleasantries exchanged in that melodic argot that was a *lingua franca* down here. He glanced at the paper in his hand and saw a letter, from the Royal Academy of Music, years ago. He would have resented this interruption, years ago. But years ago he would have spent an afternoon like this on the Steinway. So now he returned the letter to its cardboard folder and placed the folder back on the packing case and walked from one bay window to the other as the interloper approached.

A woman, of course, with greying hair spreading round the hood of her red raincoat. The raincoat could have been worn by a teenage girl, and the woman was slight of frame, like a teenage girl, but no longer young. Fifty, he would have thought, though maybe older, as she vanished from his sight and he heard the clunk of the bicycle against the portico pillar and the footsteps pausing at the doorway.

He expected to hear the bell. But no bell came.

It was late in the mask-wearing craze, and so she wondered, waiting by the door, watching the mottled figure walking slowly through the glass, would she wear one. Consideration, she could explain to him, his age being the critical one. But she knew inside herself it was a simple disguise. She had two in her pocket, a blue medical one and the designer version, decorated with tiny red and yellow fishes, that made it less like a covid mask, more, at least she hoped, like a scarf. Johnny Depp had just begun his court case against that actress with the small, adorable dog, one of whom shat in his bed, and while she knew nothing much more of the details of the case, she had to admire those shrouds they both wore, entering and leaving the courtroom, waving to their separate groups of fans. Like a more elegant version of purdah, she thought, while she hooked the elastic of the designer fishy one around her ears and finally rang the bell.

Do eyes change over the years, she wondered, and when the door finally creaked open, she realized his had not. Still the same watery blue. Still the same rather bemused abstract gaze that assumed the glance of the beholder would recognize him, not the other way round.

Women, and most particularly attractive women, conveyed an immediate sense of the familiar to him. It was a feeling of knowing, of the possibility of knowing. And she had that immediate familiarity to her. Maybe it was the red hood, the dampish blonde hair that it was hiding.

Come out from under that shell, he would remember thinking, as if the coat was an acorn and she was the edible nut beneath.

But she was too old for these kinds of ruminations, he realized as the hood slipped down. And there was that mask. Dark blue, with a pattern of dolphins. Or tiny whales. Or maybe even goldfish.

"Hello."

The word was innocent enough. It conveyed neither invitation nor its opposite. It was just there.

It kind of hung, in the dusty afternoon air.

"I hope I'm not interrupting…?"

"Not at all."

And he smiled.

The effect of that smile on her was immediate. A perceptible blush that could be seen over the dancing fishes.

"It's that time in the afternoon when any interruption is welcome. Don't you think?"

He stood aside, gracefully, despite his troubled knees.

"Let me put my mask on."

And he wished, suddenly, he had something other than that blue pharmaceutical crushed thing. Like a Kleenex, with string.

"It's for both of us, they say."

"Come in."

"No, there's no need, really. But it's about the ad you left, in Culleton's."

"Yes. A housekeeper."

And he pulled the door open now, and gestured her inside. She had no option but to enter.

"As you can see, I could do with one."

"How many days a week?"

"Two? Maybe three? Tuesdays, Thursdays? The odd weekend? If I have guests?"

"Guests," she said. "Of course. Well, I might be happy to take you up on that."

Take you up on that, he thought. As if his handwritten advert was an invitation.

And she moved, now, through the bare living room and brushed a familiar finger across the piano lid. She lifted the finger, bleached in pale dust.

"The place could do with a dusting."

"Now?" he asked, with a slight smile playing around the creases of his eyes.

She had to imagine the lips below. She wondered were they thin and cracked now, with pale traces of old man saliva round the corners. If there were, I could clean them too, she thought.

"No, of course not now. Thursday, maybe. I could bring some cleaning things."

"There's a scullery beyond the kitchen. With an assortment of utensils."

"I suppose you'd better show me then. But—" she added, as he moved towards the half-open, peeling door. "You'd better tell me how much."

"How much? I'm terrible at numbers. Better you tell me."

"What it's worth?"

"To you."

What I'm worth, she thought to herself. Twelve euro an hour, for piano lessons.

"Fifteen?" she hazarded. "An hour?"

"Fifteen pounds?"

"Yes, but in euro," she said and couldn't believe she was saying it. Here she was, bargaining. "You're in Ireland, remember?"

"Ireland, of course. Well, would twenty be reasonable?"

Reason, she thought, has nothing to do with it. She was not bargaining now, she was cheating. But she nodded her head in agreement, as she followed him into the kitchen, past the deal table with its array of uncleaned cups into the small cubby hole beyond, lit by a single beam of sunlight through the high window. There were buckets there, unused mops and J-cloths hanging from an array of probably well-rusted nails.

"And the cooking?" she asked.

"I'm on a diet," he said. "The benefits of which have yet to be revealed to me. No dairy."

"What's the problem?"

"Psoriasis," he said. "Some variant of arthritis."

"Can hit the best of us," she said.

And to her amazement he held out his hands. There was a word for the way he stretched them towards her. Proffered, she remembered. He seemed to want them touched. By her.

Those long fingers, blotched by peeling skin. She could picture the left hand still, coursing effortlessly over the lower notes in the Ravel concerto. She remembered the feel of those fingers, so long ago, in the Brighton hotel. And she touched them now, wondering would the skin remember what his rheumy eyes so obviously did not.

"Must be hard, for a pianist."

"Yes, I was a pianist once. You knew that?"

"The piano inside. Was a kind of hint."

"Those days are over. Unless, of course, the diet works."

"What's the diet?"

"No dairy. A daily mouthful of Burt's something or other."

"Burt's Bees?"

"Maybe. I keep it in the fridge."

The fridge. She would have had to check it sometime. So she moved away from those flaking hands and pulled the handle.

It opened with a subdued hiss. Like some organism inside was exhaling. She was almost afraid to look, but knelt down to examine the neon-lit interior.

It was less an affront than she had feared. A row of dark bottles, which could have been the aforementioned Burt's Bees, some curling, tired vegetables, a bag of dried lettuce. A jar of mustard.

"It could do with a clean-up."

"That would be so kind."

"And I could keep it filled, if you would give me a list."

"A list?"

"Of things not to fill it with."

She closed the door. And kind of grimaced at him. She was suddenly glad of her face covering.

"Your diet."

"Ah. Of course. Shall I make it now?"

"No," she said. "The morning will do."

"You'll be back tomorrow?"

"Have to start sometime, don't I?"

And she moved towards the door.

"A woman's work…"

She didn't feel the need to finish the phrase. She closed the door behind herself, rebalanced her bicycle and made her way down the avenue.

… is never done, she thought. No, nothing ever really finishes. In work, if that's what she could call her new situation, or in life.

4

How strange, that the same being who commented on the smallness of her hands at the age of fifteen, proffered his own hands to her – that word again – six years later, and even later again explored her body with his own, should now be watching her, from the curved bay window of the rectory as she cycled towards the gates. And watching her he was, she was sure of that. She confirmed it when she dismounted by the gates and turned back, in the act of pulling the right-hand one open. The shadow by the bay window turned away as if stung. And it couldn't have been by the sound of the creaking gate. No, it was the gaze, returned.

But maybe none of us are the same being, she mused, as she cycled on home. What had she in common with the girl who once cycled down Marino to her piano lessons in Fairview? In the upstairs apartment beyond the cinema, the rather austere refugee from East Germany who sat with his pet cockerel as she played through her scales. There were birds in common, a cockerel for him, and for her, whoever she was now, a parrot, but little else. If there was a God, she mused on, how could the woman she was now be held accountable for the failings of the girl she was then? And how could he, William Barrow, be held accountable for the sins, be they of omission or action, of his younger self? She remembered sitting in the Marie Stopes clinic in Wimbledon, staring at the brightly coloured posters on the walls behind the smiling nurses. And about that memory, enough was enough, she felt. Neither he nor she could be held to account for the outcome. And maybe his memories of her were closer to the actual, lived reality. He judged a young girl's competition, and surely forgot her. He held her hands some years later, and forgot her in turn. And the woman he slept with elicited memories of neither of their predecessors. And the ageing woman he had just hired was a different woman again. She was four different beings, passing through his life. Only he remained the same. And why was that? Fame, like memory, becomes its own connective tissue.

And he, when she caught his glance through the window while closing the distant gate, turned away as if stung. Why was that, he wondered, as he returned to the cone of dust around the unpacked case. He had a memory, sure enough, but it was the memory of desire. He recognized the frisson that her red raincoat had awoken. And perhaps he needed company more than a housekeeper. But what he hadn't expected were those slim legs, underneath the coat a much younger girl could have worn. The agility with which she swung herself onto the bike and made her way in childish figures of eight past the potholes on the avenue. He made a mental note to get them fixed and made another mental note to tell her about it.

He went to bed that evening remembering desire. The decades where it seemed like a moral failing to live without it. He remembered the onset of the AIDS crisis, the advice from the health services to catalogue one's sexual partners. He had taken out a pen and paper and begun to write.

There were so many he couldn't count. He began in his late teens with his first love and remembered each fumble up to when fame hit. From then on an explosion, with the faces blurring into one another, suspended by intervals of remembered affairs, five of them lasting long enough to be called relationships. One marriage. But the attempt at cataloguing was useless – then her – and oh god her – and several hims – it was the seventies after all. So he gave up the attempt and took an AIDS test. If the results were positive, what should he do? Place an ad in *The Times* or the *Guardian*? Anyone who remembers sleeping with William Barrow please contact the following number? He discussed this option with his therapist, who advised a deep breath and patience. And when the envelope from the hospital came he took one very deep breath. The results were negative, of course, or else he wouldn't be here, would he? He burnt the envelope, the catalogue, and vowed to change his ways.

And perhaps now the reader doesn't like him. But that is an emotion shared, rather oddly, on waking the next morning, by William Barrow. He had never liked himself. He had stood before the mirror in his mother's bedroom and looked at his naked shape from behind, and decided he didn't like what he saw. Should a boy's bare bum be shaped like double apples? Or maybe that awkward form was just the chrysalis, waiting for the glorious butterfly to emerge. He had avoided mirrors after that. He had practised like a demon, as if trying to carve out another personality, force another being from his own skin. And when the prizes began, when William Barrow's name was called from yet another podium in another dusty hall, the figure that ascended the wooden steps was this being, this avatar, separate from him. And with each success this being seemed to grow, assume its own postures, its own way of walking, even its own thoughts. And he came to realize that he, whoever he was, had to accommodate himself to this emergent William Barrow. He was helped in this accommodation by the diffidence of his middle-class London home. Richmond, the Victorian streets curving down towards the park. His mother a violin teacher, his father a vet, whose alarm at the development of his rather driven son was soothed by his devotion to the dogs of the neighbourhood. Basset hounds, Alsatians, mutts of each and every variety rewarded his attentions with a simple affection that he always found lacking in William.

So William Barrow, WB, emerged as a public thing in painful stages, like a second, endlessly prolonged birth, forced into being by those elegant long fingers, hours of practice on the upright in the Richmond house, on the Steinway in the Parry Rooms, overlooking the Albert Hall, on his silent clavier, when his international career began in earnest. William Barrow, WB, was in all significant ways brought into being by those hands, his escape from himself was orchestrated by those fingers and he only had to meet himself again when those hands became a problem.

It began in his early sixties, the decade that should have formed the summation of his career. On the palms, at first. Rough accretions of skin led to bleeding cracks, flakes and pustules between the fingers, then it spread to the wrists, to the nails themselves. He had numerous consultations, so many he came to hate the thought of a dermatologist's waiting room, another prescription for a corticoid ointment, leafing through another beauty magazine behind women waiting for yet another Botox appointment. The only male at the mercy of a practice devoted almost entirely to women, he came to loathe the blue- and green-smocked practitioners with their false smiles and their promises of expert medical advice. His hands seemed as much an embarrassment to them as they were to him, when they scraped skin samples and tweezered them into sealed plastic bags. What they really wanted was a woman in her mid-thirties, whose lines needed periodic adjustment, not this ageing concert pianist whose hands had begun to flake and fail. And their final judgement was delivered with something like relief. He had psoriatic arthritis, with plaque complications, a condition incurable, but manageable, with certain treatments. He could lead a fully functioning active life, unless the condition led to arthritis mutilans, a remote possibility. He could walk, cycle, swim, even garden, with the help of gardening gloves. But as a concert pianist, he was finished.

And so began his reacquaintance with himself. Music had abandoned him, but who remained when it had gone? Or what?

It was an interesting question, and although he didn't ask it, in that exactly rhetorical sense, to himself, in an odd way he found himself living it. He found the ageing, crabbed, tall being he saw in the mirror each morning to be a stranger, but a not uninteresting one. If he had seen him, swaying amongst other bodies on the tube, he might even have envied him. The thinning hair, still thick, despite the flecks of grey, the shoulders, not yet stooped, the stomach flat, beneath the waistcoat, or what Susannah for some reason had insisted on calling the "vest". A somewhat old-fashioned garment that he couldn't quite explain his attachment to. Only the lean can wear one, or wear one properly. It accentuated his height somehow, and his attachment to an era, not only of fashion, but of music too, long past. Old-fashioned. He was old-fashioned, in musical and sartorial tastes, but the waistcoat somehow suited this house, too warm most months for a jacket, too breezy for shirt-sleeves. The vest, as Susannah again would have called it, was perfect. Warmed the torso, left the wrists and hands free. If only he could play.

Another question. Music. Did he really miss it? He had been seduced, he realized, in his early teens, then married for decades, to a beauty who returned his devotion with a chilly kind of absence, bemusement and contempt. And now that he could no longer play, he understood what the source of the bemusement was. He played the notes, he allowed his perfect fingers to inhabit the worlds of their arrangements, he spent his days in a maze of ascending melodies and arpeggios that were dreamed by someone else. As a working pianist, the irony had never bothered him, but as an ageing retiree from the concert stage, with only the memory of those notes to occupy his hours, he could see how pathetic his ambitions were. He had played, dutifully, rigorously, perfectly, even, but had invented nothing. He had elicited waves of applause, in concert halls from New York to Bratislava, and now, with his absence from that circuit, someone else would take his place, with a marginally different version of the Chopin or of the Busoni arrangement of Bach's *Partita in D Minor*.

D Moll. He remembered the German, and the hint of exoticism that word gave rise to, when he first saw it on the manuscript page. He must have been close to nine, then. In the living room of the house in Richmond, with the upright piano facing the wet square. It was for the left hand, he remembered, Brahms had managed another transcription, and now that he remembered it, his left hand was somewhat better than his right. He began to search amongst the half-opened boxes for the sheet music, and then realized he remembered it without them.

He sank into the piano stool, unstretched his left hand and began to press, ever so gently, the keys. The first chord sounded out, declarative, despite the tiny pressure his fingers could exert. Then the variations on the same, and the beginnings of that melody, in a descending scale that had the authority of something hewn from ancient, Germanic wood. Bach had written in memory of his dead wife, so the legend went, but what was so magnificent was the lack of personality, of individuation to the development. It followed on with the inevitability of time, of mathematics, of an endless game of chess, towards a conclusion that had the stillness of a placid lake or a quiet grave.

5

And was it then, or later, when the arpeggios began, that he realized he wasn't alone? He turned slowly, his left hand fingering the broken chords, and saw her to his right, in the shadow of the alcove of the doorway, two supermarket bags in her hand. The same fish-patterned mask on her face.

"The door," she said, with a hint of muffled apology in her voice, "was open."

"Of course," he said.

"Maybe I should have knocked?"

"Or I could get you a key cut?"

"But then if I had knocked, I wouldn't have heard."

"Heard?"

"Your hands work. You can still play."

"Just the left one," he said, and began to rub the left hand with the right. "Maybe it's the sunshine."

And he reached his hand out into the strip of sunlight that was coming through the bay window.

"And I wouldn't call that playing."

"Sounded like playing. To my untutored ear."

And she had a strange urge, standing there, in the alcove, her own hands weighed down with the SuperValu bags. To take his hand in hers, massage it back to some kind of health. Ridiculous,

32

she thought. Get a handle on yourself. So she reached one foot back against the half-opened front door and heard it click closed. She realized her knee was showing. And for some reason she didn't care.

"You bought some things?"

"Messages," she said.

"Messages," he repeated.

"That's what we call it. You probably call it shopping."

"Groceries. I hope you kept receipts?"

"I did. You can pay me for them later."

"Messages," he repeated again.

"From when your mother," she said, and she entered the room fully, heading for the kitchen and the safety of the fridge, "scribbled a note and sent you to the shops."

"And they were the messages?"

"The notes were the messages. And what the grocer gave you kind of – became the messages—"

"How odd."

"Odd," she says. "And Irish. Small differences."

"Are there others?"

"There are."

She clumped across the room. Her heels sounded unwieldy on the bare boards.

"What you call Boxing Day—"

"After Christmas?"

"We call Saint Stephen's."

She stopped, between the piano and the packing cases. The wooden kind, with strips of metal round the edges. How long had they been there, she wondered?

"I got cleaning stuff and rubber gloves and some of that Burt's Bees you seem to need."

"And the receipts?"

"Have them here."

She placed the crumpled receipts on the piano cover. He noticed her blunt hand, reddened with either the cold outside or too much detergent. She stood apart from him and pulled on a pair of rubber gloves. Pale and stretchable that made the hands look like two jellyfish, swimming against the dark Steinway. She reached out a rubber forefinger and trailed it through the quiet film of grey.

"Needs dusting."

"I'm sure. I've hardly touched it since—"

"But you're playing now. I'll start in the kitchen."

"You mean the scullery," he said.

"So, it's not a kitchen yet?"

"There is a difference?"

"Depends on what you use it for."

She moved then, across the bare varnished boards, carrying the bags with her. For some reason he was aware of every step. She touched the boards with her heel first, he noticed, and afterwards with the sole so each step sounded like a wooden heartbeat. Or successive beats on a kettle drum. He stretched his left hand again to continue with the partita but either the sense of congealing tension was gathering again, or she was creating a rhythmic distraction. The sound of her heels, callump, off the floorboards became a staccato echoing clap on the flagstones of the scullery. Or the kitchen, as he realized he would now have to call it.

She had reached the fridge now. The metal door opened with its forbidding hiss.

He closed the piano lid, stood, in his trainers and his mismatched socks, with the tweed trousers and the waistcoat above them, and stretched his crabbed hands. He heard a series of joints unclicking, which could have been a cousin to the sounds of her heels on the scullery flagstones. He would take a walk, he decided. In the garden behind. But to make an exit through the front door, past the front house windows and round by the small cramped ones of the scullery would have seemed indelicate, somehow. A small trek of avoidance. The most obvious path was to the arch of the scullery, over the flagstones and out the small door. Why did he even care, he wondered? He would have had to pass her, bent over the lowest shelf of the open fridge door. She was already falling to her knees. A small hand towel, he noticed, to protect them against the stone.

So he turned, trod by the piano once more and was heading for the front steps when something held him there. Her soft humming, maybe, and the rhythmic scrape of the brush against the stone. The unemptied packing cases sat in a patch of sunlight, below one of the windows. Maybe it was time to admit that he lived nowhere but here.

And he was wrenching the lid off one of them when he heard her voice again.

"Enough playing?"

"For the moment."

"What a pity," she said.

"Why?"

"Music while you work—"

"You want to hear more?"

"Love to."

He could see her calves, and the arches of her heels, with the sandals flapping free of them. And he saw, inside the packing case, a stack of his own records. He removed the sleeve from a Chopin and placed it on the turntable.

35

"Chopin," she said. Her head was obscured by the mottled glass of the kitchen door. Her calves shifting with the scrubbing.

"You know it?"

"One of the ballades."

"Which one?" he asked.

"Don't know," she said.

Yet somehow, obscurely, he felt she did. He walked quietly to the kitchen door, watching her, almost in a yoga pose, with the outstretched palms.

"Number one," he said. "In G minor."

She felt his shadow then, and turned. And gasped with fright, almost upsetting the bucket beside her.

"I'm sorry," he said.

The music still echoed around them.

"It wasn't you playing?"

"It was me. Some time ago."

"It's a record?" she asked.

"Forgive me. I found it amongst my unpacked things."

"It's beautiful," she said. "But you—"

"I frightened you. My apologies again. It's just so odd to listen to one's younger self."

He held out his hands again. Began to knead the fingers.

"You shouldn't be unpacking with those hands."

"No?"

"Dust mites. Fabrics. I'll do it for you. Tomorrow."

"You'll unpack my life?"

"You're paying, aren't you?"

"Yes," he said. "I'm paying. Happily. Fifteen euro an hour."

"Twenty," she said, and felt an odd pang of guilt. Had she tricked him into that number?

"Twenty," he said. "Of course."

6

So she unpacked his life. Not that day, or the next, but two days afterwards. It was odd the way she longed to get back there. She couldn't understand her own feelings, as if the house had a dark magnetic attraction. She gave the sticky Brian one more lesson, had two more sessions with the blonde-haired twins, daughters of the industrialist who had a house in nearby Schull, then cancelled all further teaching.

"Why?" Mary Culleton asked her, since the mother of Brian, red-haired and every bit as unlovely as her unwashed son, had come to the coffee shop in tears.

"Why do you think?" Tara asked, more brusquely than she intended.

"Covid? You've underlying health conditions?"

"No. I'm as healthy as a trout. It's just. You can't trust kids to keep their hands clean. I'm sick of washing down those piano keys."

"You'll be taking the PUP?"

"What's the deal with that?"

"If you lose income because of the corona, you can claim it."

"No. I've got other work."

"Where?"

And her eyes must have inadvertently flashed to the

noticeboard. The announcement. Dangling askew now on its single pin.

Wanted.
Housekeeper.
Possible cooking duties.

"You're working for him?"
"Wouldn't call it work."
"Oh my god. Is this like a—"
"Like nothing. It's work."
"A secret?"
"No secret. I clean the house. Do some cooking. Shopping. Unpack his things."
"And does he play? Music while you work?"
"Can't. The hands. Psoriasis."
"God love him. I did see the hands."
"Shouldn't be near water. Detergent. Dust mites."
"So he leaves that up to you?"
"Pays me for it."
"Go for it, Tara. Unpack him."

As she parked her bicycle to the side, by the peeling pillar, she wondered was that what she was doing. Unpacking him. Stripping him down to his essentials, to find out what's left. Or peeling him down, like an artichoke, to find the heart. And what then? Eating it whole? Or dicing it into consumable segments? And if that was what she was up to, she wondered how long it would take.

She attacked the cases that afternoon. She needed his help, to sort one thing from another. The clothes, first, which he seemed a little embarrassed about. Three camphor-smelling monkey suits, one with full tails.

"You need these for your concerts?"

"Certain of them."

She brushed the dust off one of them. Remembered it, the shape, as he took a bow. But couldn't remember, was it the Wigmore Hall or the Brighton Dome?

"There's the wardrobe in the spare room upstairs. I'll put them there."

"I could sell them. Or give them to a charity shop."

"Why?"

And for some reason the thought was like a slap in the face. To her. And when she dared a look, she saw it was to him as well. There was a blur in his eyes, above the mask. Like tears.

"I doubt I'll need them in the future."

"You never know."

"Besides, they're somewhat… old-fashioned now."

"Don't concert pianists wear dress-suits?"

"It's no longer de rigueur. In fact, some of the younger female set could be dressed in Victoria's Secret."

"Underwear?"

"Almost. A bare waist. Slashed midriff. Bondage gear. Whatever causes a sensation."

"Isn't the music enough?"

"My dear."

He blinked, and rubbed his eyes.

"Was the music ever enough?"

She laid the dress-suits over the bare couch. Album after album then, above a row of equally stiff dress-shoes. She heard him sneeze.

"I'm raising a storm, amn't I?"

He smiled. He liked that "amn't I".

"That's another of those," he said.

"Of what?"

"Irishisms. Like messages. I would have said, aren't I?"

"The question was, is the dust bothering you? You could leave this business to me."

"And do what?"

"What? Play the piano."

"I can't."

"Then go for a walk. Or something."

Odd again, she thought. The repartee, almost bickering. As if they'd known each other for years. Which in a way they had. Though how was he to know that?

She watched him walk, backwards, arms gently raised as if against the dust, and turn into the scullery. She heard the scrape of the kitchen door opening.

He was smiling, when he came out the door, down the mossy steps, into the unweeded garden. He unhooked the mask, dangled it between his fingers, and saw himself in the window, as the door closed, the unfamiliar creases on his own lips, which vanished the moment he became aware of them.

Did he need a gardener too, he wondered? Another notice stuck to the board by the freezer in the café? Maybe his hands could manage the weeds, as a kind of substitute for the music. He walked through the grass, kicking away the briars that tried to wrap round his trainers. They almost had a life of their own. And had reached a patch of dew-damp grass, which the briars for some reason left untangled, when the ground gave way beneath him.

It was the briars, ironically, that saved him, spreading from the roots of an old hawthorn tree. The grass collapsing, like a green soufflé, his feet, his knees, even his hips sinking downwards, and if he hadn't managed to grab an intergrown rope of thorned blackberry, he would have vanished. Into where, he wondered? Maybe it was time to vanish. But they ripped his palms bloody and slowed his descent. He ended up with his elbows jammed against the semi-circle of grass that remained unbroken, his legs dangling into some abyss below. And he closed his palms around the rope of thorned blackberry and began to pull.

It was as if the briars wanted him up, the grass and the mud beneath it wanted him down, into that black pit that children dream about. He scrabbled with his trainers against whatever surface they touched and miraculously found a hold. And together with whatever indent the toes of his trainers found and with the briared blackberry rope his bloody hands clutched at, he managed to painfully squirm back onto solid ground.

His knees settled on a stretch of undisturbed grass and he felt secure enough to let go. But the thorns clung to his palms like tiny fish hooks. He managed one hand free, and then the other, and thought of picking the thorns out with his teeth. He realized the absurdity of the thought and rested both knuckles on the grass, breathing in huge gulps of air, conscious of little else but his thumping heart. And then slowly, like a frightened child, he gathered the courage to turn. The grass beneath him still felt treacherous, as if some other volcanic event could propel him to the heavens or drag him down below. He could see a semi-circle of dark, where the earth had collapsed. He squirmed round on his elbows, managed to get his face to where his feet had been and stared down into the abyss below.

And he felt it again, that shiver of childhood terror. The dark, between the floorboard and the mattress. The shadows the beech tree made on the lintel of his bedroom window. The flecks of black when he closed his childhood eyes.

There was a long cylinder of shade leading to a pool of water, far, far below. Tangles of grass at the broken lip and an echo of luminescent green clinging to the descendant, curved walls. The gleam of that iridescent wetness, the only illumination, apart from the pale daylight above, which shifted with the movement of his head. And everywhere, those shadows.

He managed to stand then, conscious of his breathing and his thumping heart. He walked back slowly through the briars, stepping above and around them, as if terrified that some other natural element would have its way with him. And when he made it through the scullery door, his uneasiness, if anything, increased.

She wasn't there.

He should have been relieved, and he felt foolish not to be, as he placed his hands above the sink and relished the flow of cold water. The bleeding began to ease, but there were the gouges the thorns had left. And the broken thorns themselves. He needed tweezers, a pin, an antiseptic cream and hadn't a clue where to find them.

He made his way to the living room and she wasn't there either. The disappointment hit him again, and began to feel like panic. He would have called out but realized, stupidly, that he didn't know her name. He made his way up the stairs, wondering what else he didn't know. And he found her in the upstairs spare bedroom, the one looking out on the front lawns with the meandering drive and the elm and poplar trees. She was closing the door to the wardrobe and her mask had slipped.

She turned, when the door clattered open, and pulled it up, as if it was a towel that hid her nakedness. She was about to blush, when she saw the bleeding hands.

"What have you done?" she asked.

"Not sure," he said. He walked towards her and proffered

both hands this time. That was the only word for it, she would realize later. It had a religious aura to it. What else does one proffer? Bread, at mealtime. The host, at communion. A gift, at Christmas.

"My god."

The thorns shocked her. They looked like dark nails in the grey smudges of his palms.

"Here."

She took his right hand between hers, led him into the bathroom, turned the tap and held it underneath the flowing water.

"Already done that—"

"Maybe, but—"

"I need a what's it called—"

"Tweezers," she said, and reached into the cabinet above. She found what she should have expected. Nothing.

"Here—"

She took a safety pin from her apron and began to probe. Now was the moment, she realized, if she wanted him to feel pain. But his eyes stayed on hers with a mute, acceptant trust. It was almost annoying. Why on earth should he trust her, this apparent stranger? Someone should have taught him to be more circumspect. His mother, maybe?

She edged one thorn to the surface of his skin, and then another.

"Close your eyes," she said.

"Why?" he asked, stupidly.

"OK, don't. Then turn away."

And when he did so, obediently, she pulled down the mask, brought his palm to her mouth and used her teeth to finish the job.

43

She spat the thorns out into the flowing water, pulled the mask back up, then repeated the process on his left hand.

"Does it hurt?" she asked.

"Not at all," he answered.

"Men," she said. "Just admit it does."

"OK, it does. Just a little."

She did better with the pin on this hand. No teeth needed. She placed that too under the flowing water, then wrapped a towel round them both.

He looked like a prisoner, manacled by linen. She bent down to the canvas bag at her feet and came up with a small bottle of antiseptic.

"You just happened to have that with you?" he asked, stupidly, once more.

"No," she answered, "I kind of knew you'd gouge yourself with thorns."

He realized he was meant to laugh at this, and managed a smile.

"So, how did you do this? It's not really the time of year for picking blackberries."

"I'd better show you."

"Show me?"

"In case you happen to fall in."

She followed him then, down the stairs, through the kitchen/ scullery, out the door to what must have once been a garden. Through the tangle of briars, around the old bent hawthorn, to the collapsed, and now almost perfect, circular hole in the ground.

"A well," she said.

"It must have been," he answered. "Once."

"I suppose every big house needed one. Although—"

44

She stepped closer, and he touched her elbow. Gently, then, drew her back.

"Careful."

"Sorry."

She turned towards him.

"It seems older than the house, somehow."

"How can you tell?"

"The moss. The old stone. There was a legend about—"

She stopped herself. She didn't even know why she had said that. A soft breeze rustled through the orchard, but couldn't even tremor the branches of that hawthorn. As if they had seen too many years.

"A legend?"

"In the townland. The parish."

Why did she use that word? What did she know about the parish? Another exotic Irishism, like messages. Still, it was fun to probe his gullibility. That hole in the ground seemed to need an explanation. And it did give some substance to her next conjecture.

"Did I hear it or read about it? About a saint's well. That—"

"That what?"

"I don't remember really. Something about moss. And water. That you know. Cured boils and things."

He looked at the back of his hands in the pale sunlight. Then turned to look at the damaged palms.

"You'll need to make it safe. Cover it up. Or fence it off."

"I'll need someone to help with that."

She sank to her knees on the wet grass.

"Careful—"

She peered downwards. Clutched two clumps of grass with either hand.

"Let me think, she said. I might know just the lad—"

Though he wasn't a lad. And she wondered would he have been waiting for her call.

"You said there was a legend—"

"Did I?"

She stood then, carefully.

"Just came into my head. There's all sorts of shite talked about—"

"Shite?"

"You know. Every stone and bush around."

"Old wives' tales?"

"Hey," she said. And she turned and caught his eye. "I'm not that old."

"My apologies."

She wondered about Peter, cycling home. What a call from her might imply. The thought of his hand on hers once more made her shiver. But. She knew they would have to meet sometime. And there was that idle curiosity about what he had been up to. So she Skyped him that evening and agreed to meet him outside Culleton's for coffee the next morning.

"It's a hole in the ground," she told him. "In the gardens of the old rectory. Some kind of well. Himself almost tumbled in—"

"Himself?"

She was warming her fingers on the cardboard cup, blowing the foam from the surface.

"I'm cleaning his house. The piano boy."

"Hardly a boy, Tara."

It was odd to hear her name again on his lips.

"No, he's not young anymore. Anyway, there's a collapsed

46

hole in an old vegetable garden that needs making safe. You can charge him by the hour."

"Like you do?"

She nodded. Took a sip.

"Twenty euro an hour," she said. "I'm sure you could charge more."

"What do you think it needs? Covering up? A JCB, a few tons of earth—"

"It'd be a shame," she said, "to cover it up."

"Why?"

"It's old," she said. "Maybe ancient. It might have some – what's the word?"

"Archaeological?"

"That's it. Significance."

"There's a story there?"

"Maybe there is. If someone could find it."

When she cycled up the next day, she was surprised to see his white HiAce van already in the forecourt. There was a presumption to its presence there that irritated her. Why, she wasn't even sure. She could see his shadow through the bay window, which only increased her irritation. And when she had made her way inside and saw him maskless by the piano, all the fury of their relationship returned.

"Mask, Peter," she said.

"He didn't ask for it. And, I haven't got one."

"Here."

She took a blue medical one from her pocket and almost threw it towards him. He caught it, deftly, between two strong fingers before it hit the floor.

"Where is he?"

Peter shrugged. He had always been good at shrugging.

"The door was open. Someone called me to walk in. And so, I'm waiting—"

Two of us, she thought. And, while waiting, she walked over to the piano and pressed a random set of keys.

"So, you play?" She heard and immediately withdrew her hands.

He was at the top of the stairs, buttoning the same waistcoat.

"Not only plays," Peter interjected. "She teaches, too."

"How unexpected," he said, as he descended. "And this is?"

"Peter," she said.

"McConnell," Peter said.

"He can fix your hole," she said. And unfortunately, it sounded funny.

"In the ground," Peter said. And her irritation increased, if that was possible. Did he think she was referring to his anus?

"William," he said, as he came closer. "Forgive me if I don't shake. And why don't we have a look?"

The sun came out, as they approached it. It silhouetted the outline of the hawthorn tree. And for some reason it enhanced the darkness below the broken circle of grass. As if the shadows hid something.

"I could fill it in," Peter offered, "if you wouldn't mind a JCB coming through the brambles."

"No," she said, and, again, wasn't sure why she said it.

"Why not?" William asked.

"Because of the story," she said.

"There's a story?"

"A whatdoyoucallit."

"A legend?"

"Yep. I'm looking into it."

"You are?"

This from Peter.

"Something about a well. In the townland. A saint attached."

"Never heard of it."

Again, from Peter.

"Well, you wouldn't have, would you?"

"And you would?"

William looked from one to the other. And she wanted done with the conversation.

"You could fence it off. Save churning up the gardens. And the well."

"And the story?"

"Save that too."

"If there is one—"

And Peter now walked in a wider circle round the circular hole.

"A fence," he said. "What manner of fence?"

"Some kind of wooden thing. None of your barbed wire business."

"Wooden stakes. Need a bunch of them."

"You'd get them in that place beyond Bantry. Future Forests. And a trellis—"

"I'll pick them out myself?"

There was a silence. And what seemed like a soft breath, from the well below.

"Maybe you'd come with me?"

She nodded. She had led herself into this. She had to wonder, for the first time, why she felt so proprietorial.

"With his permission—"

She looked at William. And was strangely relieved when he nodded.

7

There was the drive, then, to Bantry, in the HiAce van. The smell of squashed cigarettes, of engine oil, of something like fish scales.

"Where are you living these days?"

"I sleep on the boat."

So that's where it came from. Smell seemed too mean a word. The odour.

"You have a boat?"

"Tara, how much do you know about me?"

"Oh, of course. The boat. Knew you fished one. Didn't know it was yours."

"Tell me the story, then."

"The story?"

"The legend."

And she began to realize the real function of her invention. It was a strategy of avoidance. Safer to invent a tale than to address whatever was left between them.

"Some kind of saint."

"What kind of saint?"

"She had a blemish on her face."

"A blemish?"

"Her cheek. Like your man in Russia."

"Putin?"

"No, the one before him. Gorbachev."

"Ah, a port-wine stain. On his head—"

"Hers was on her cheek. All over. Both cheeks."

"She was a saint?"

"Not a saint then, when she discovered the well. But it wasn't a well yet."

"A spring?"

"Yep. And she was staring into the water below when a boy came up behind her."

"A shepherd?"

"Something like that. Or a goatherd. Startled her, so she fell in."

"And she drowned?"

"No, the goatherd pulled her out."

"And?"

"He saw the blemish on her face. Found her so ugly, he did a runner."

She was enjoying the elaboration of the tale.

"You're not making this up?"

"Not at all."

"But I have to admit, even if you are—"

He slowed the van, as a tractor pulled from a side road.

"I have to admit, it's good—"

"The next day, she woke up, and the blemish was gone."

"From her cheeks?"

"Both of them. The same goatherd sees her in the marketplace. Thinks she's the most beautiful vision he has ever seen. Thinks it's the first time he's seen her. And she realizes that her blemish was a useful disguise. Kind of like a mask. Kept her safe from the whatdoyoucallit."

"What?"

"The male gaze."

And he looked at her as he drove. Traced the profile of her body with his eyes.

"Like this one?"

"Maybe."

"So what does she do?"

"She gives him the brush-off. She devotes herself to the well. The waters. The healing powers. People came from all around. Then, in the summer, the water dried up."

"Shit. So that was it?"

"No. She gathered the moss from the stonework. And she found it had even more."

"Healing powers?"

"Yes."

"Has she a name?"

"Yes. Ite."

"Ita?" he asked. "With an 'a'?"

"No. Ite. With an 'e'."

"Tara," he said. They were pulling through the wooded entrance to Future Forests.

She recognized the tone. She wondered how she'd deal with it.

"Do you miss me?"

"The way I miss cigarettes. I know they're bad for me."

"You want one?"

He pulled a packet from the dashboard, placed one between his lips.

"No," she said. "But you go ahead."

They chose a type of sharpened wooden stake and some seemingly elastic yards of trellis. She had to wonder at the construction of it, as she watched Peter stretch and squeeze it, like a melodeon. She bought herself a pair of gardening gloves and helped him wrangle the lot into the back of the HiAce van. It began to feel dangerously like companionship, so she left him back in the rectory with the jumble of staves, trellis and garden implements by the black hole amongst the brambles. The one he had taken to calling "her pianist" was nowhere to be seen.

8

And as she cycled back she began to wonder. Where the very idea of the tall tale had come from. It was fun, of course, to probe his gullibility. But it had leapt unbidden into the half-aware bits of her brain, like a frog from a rainy pond. Or the waters of a well, would you believe. And where did that would you believe itself come from? Her internal monologue was turning into some maiden aunt's. She had had a Catholic girlhood, like everyone else in Drumcondra the suburb she had grown up in. Whitworth Road, in the shadow of Croke Park. What she had hated most were the match Sundays, whole streets closed down to traffic, Kerry policemen barring the entrances and the exits. The after-match processions down to Hill 16 pub on Gardiner Street. Music afforded her the only escape, from the church incense and the droning afternoon voice of Michael O'Hehir. When she moved to London she shared a squat with a Hungarian couple and could compare their memories of weekends in Budapest with weekends in Dublin. The same brown lethargy, the same uniform conformity, the same excitement at the explosive intrusions from the great Western culture beyond. She had a dim memory of bliss at the sight of her first communion dress, but could hardly remember wearing it. She remembered no epiphanies, whatever that word meant, except when the first chords of "Parisian Walkways" sounded out from the speakers of the Grove dancehall in Raheny. And even that was more to do with the imminent contact with a boy called Sam.

Revenge, maybe, she obscurely thought, as a massive truck almost blew her sideways, coming the opposite way. She must remember to wear her hi-vis jacket. But she hadn't got the energy to work up any real fury. It was curiosity more than anything that drew her to the rectory, the same curiosity, now that she thought of it, that had always drawn her back into his orbit. I wonder what his life looks like now. And at his lack of recognition, of any acknowledgement it might bring, she was neither disappointed nor surprised. Although she had to admit, he still cut an elegant shape. Some of us are born that way, she thought, and others try to manage it. What way? Svelte was the word, as she reached the main street and then she thought, no, that applies almost exclusively to women. But it was somehow apt for him, at whatever age. Even in those trainers, those mismatched socks, that parka, sipping his herbal tea outside of Mary Culleton's. She felt the bile of a subdued anger then and wondered what he would have thought of her, in the unlikely event that he had remembered. How different she was. Like him, another person, yet mysteriously the same. And she realized there was no mystery about it. She wasn't the same.

Whatever her true feelings were, that dark pool at the bottom of the cylindrical green moss seemed a fitting reflection of them. It said nothing, but implied a multitude. She could have only caught a glimpse of it but could see it when she closed her eyes, reflecting tiny shards of broken sunlight from above. And she mustn't close her eyes, turning as she was off Main Street towards her cottage home.

She heard Erik the parrot greet her with the screech of the first bars of *Gnossienne No. 1*. She replied in kind with an answering whistle. It would hardly have made Satie happy, but it was a kind of conversation. More satisfying than most, she realized, there's a certain comfort in the absence of particular meaning to any reply. Like talking to that Dutch boyfriend she once had. What was his name? Erik as well? No, she remembered. Arl. So she walked through to the kitchen and the parrot's cage and whistled for a while to entertain him. And as she did so the thought of Amsterdam came into her head. She had gone there with Arl from Gatwick on one of those rare weekends when the canals were frozen. She had twisted her ankle on the ice-skates, which rather ruined their time together. She had to endure his lack of conversation in one of those smoke cafés with the intense odour of burning hashish adding to the communal gloom. On their way back to the hotel he kept singing his tuneless version of "Sad Eyed Lady of the Lowlands". Where the sad-eyed prophet says that no man comes. It seemed like the most mawkish attempt at poetics to her, for which, she had realized, she couldn't really blame Bob Dylan. No, she could only blame this Dutch beanpole with his sibilant attempts at English consonants. The two single beds in a cramped hotel room were hardly the best augur for continuity of the relationship, which ended soon afterwards. So why was she thinking of it now? It had come into her head, the way the story of the well did, but she had lived one experience and only imagined the other.

Ite, she said to the parrot, and then remembered the Latin in the church choir she had sung in, in that huge sanctified warehouse on the Drumcondra Road. If an aircraft hangar to Catholicism could have been built, this would have been it. With its lurid mosaics of the Stations of the Cross, the enormous echo of every cough and shuffle, the choir singing as the priest did his blessing, *Ite, missa est*. At least that's how she remembered it. And she had to wonder, why had she chosen that name?

She sank into the chair by the kitchen table and saw her computer in front of her. Wells, she typed in, and saw a stream of references to Wells Fargo and a place called Wells in Somerset. Magic wells, she typed in, which led her to holy wells and a dim memory of a walk through crutches to a rag-strewn grotto somewhere in Clare. Her mother leaned on her elbow, suffering from sciatica or rheumatism, she could hardly remember now. Her father sat in the Cortina at the end of the dry stone lane, listening to *The Sunday Game*. That voice again, Michael O'Hehir. So maybe that was where the memory came from, and she felt again her childhood confusion at that almost ceremonial array of crutches on each side, leading to the irregular stone arch. Did the crippled ones leave them there cured? Or were they a ceremonial decoration, like the marble-coloured vistas in the hangar in Drumcondra? They somehow implied a vulgar certainty in miracles. But there could be nothing vulgar about such a thing, she thought, passing two rusting wheelchairs, as her mother under the grotto arch said help me darling, bending to get a hand in the dark water. And only the water had the mystery the whole journey implied. Lapping under her mother's hand, reflecting the broken grey daylight, so low that it must have originated in the earth's underbelly. It brought a shudder of fear, rather than wonder.

Ite, the parrot squawked in return and began another series of tuneless whistles. As good a name as any, she thought, for that nameless well. She remembered again for some reason the mosaics in that draughty hangar of a church, the choir pressed round her, the distant priest stretching his arms out to tell them it was over. Then the walk down Drumcondra Road and if they were lucky an ice-cream at the corner shop. Past the Royal Canal where there was always some man doing something dodgy amongst the weeds, pissing in the waters or worse. She had kept herself free of groping hands until her first love, and she still remembered the feeling of it all falling away, on the living room carpet with the cherry trees outside. *Ite, missa est.* Something was definitely over, she thought, walking back outside, the pink blossoms falling all around. She had raised her face to greet them as she would to greet snowflakes. But they were soft and she hardly felt them. He was Sam, an apprentice electrician, and left soon afterwards to work with the wiring systems on the merchant navy. She got postcards thereafter, from Liverpool, Lee on the Solent, the Isle of Man, Gibraltar. Declarations of love, with always the date for his return, but when he came back she had outgrown him. Music had taken his place, the trek down the canal to the Fairview Cinema which had become a furniture warehouse to the upstairs flat on Marino Crescent, the East German piano teacher and his observant hen. Haltung, he would say, tapping her spine with his ruler, haltung, which she came to understand meant posture. He was worried her obsession with practice would turn her into a crabbed, unlovely thing. She was touched by his concern, more so than by the entreaties of Sam when he returned from his marine travels. He wore stickers for The Ramones on his denim jacket, took her to watch Home Farm play Bohemians and the only saving grace she could find in him was that he never asked her to Croke Park. Goodbye again, she said to him, down on the North Wall docks when he rejoined his merchant navy. The ships stank of diesel and old rope and it would always remain a mystery to her why they were given female names. There was nothing feminine about them. And all of this was before her appearance at the piano competition in the Francis Xavier Hall.

She thought about the girl who played that competition as she would think about a stranger. And maybe that was it, the key, the mystery at the bottom of the well. She was a different person. The girl who had walked her mother though those dry stone walls decorated with crutches was not the girl who lost her virginity on the living room floor of Tonlegee Road; was not the girl who rattled out her Bach fugues in front of the Rachmaninoff virtuoso, who, despite his height, the length of his strong fingers, his tweed waistcoated figure, carried a diffidence with him, an abstraction that was decidedly feminine. She should be so lucky, she remembered thinking, when she met him again in the Wigmore Hall. She was on a scholarship then, studying in St Giles by day, waitressing by night. She had cropped her hair, flaunted a nose-stud, wore unlaced Doc Martens underneath a leather skirt. She could have called herself Siouxsie, for all of the connection she had with her younger self. That he wouldn't recognize her was a given, but maybe something would be sparked by the contact with those tiny, tiny hands. She took a fluted glass of champagne from him and her fingers brushed his, and she realized nothing would.

By the time they met again, in Brighton, she was another stranger. Could have called herself Desiree, or Blaise, with her preference for bustiers, under long flowing cloaks and spiked heels. She lived in a downstairs garden flat behind the station with a bass player whose dabbling in heroin made her realize that a career in teaching and not performance might enable her at least to survive. And when she read about the piano recital in the Brighton Dome, she bought one ticket, not two. He would have affected uninterest anyway, her leather-clad devotee of Hugh Cornwell and The Stranglers, despite his graduation from the Royal Academy. So she went alone, a different person again, and was surprised to meet at the reception afterwards the same rather abstract diffidence, the same elegant hands, the same person, oddly enough, who remembered nothing of her earlier selves.

Are the ones who don't change luckier than the ones who do? But what did she know of his inner self, his subterranean movements, she wondered, as they prolonged their evening in the shabby downstairs bar of his waterfront hotel. The one that had been blown to pieces in the attempt on Margaret Thatcher, he reminded her, and he wondered how her assailants must have felt as she staggered down the staircase, out onto the Brighton promenade, her handbag still between her diamond-ringed fingers, barely a hint of plaster on her coiffed hair. Another one who barely changed, Tara mumbled, and when he questioned her she asked him was it an English quality, this persistence of form. Was she fishing, hoping for some recognition of her earlier self? No, she was genuinely curious. The way they finished their sentences, as if subject, predicate and object was an ingrained quality to the language which was, on any accounting, no longer theirs. Englishness, she told him, fascinated her almost, and she didn't tell him this, as much as he himself did. Some essence that persisted, outside the blizzard of change. They hardly own the language any more, she told him, warming to her subject. As Miles Davis said in the Albert Hall, English wasn't meant to be spoken like that. To prove your point, he told her, you'd have to be more specific. You've proved it, she replied, and ordered another drink.

There was a silent piano keyboard on the desk in his hotel room. He used it, she supposed, on long-haul flights, waiting in airport lobbies. She couldn't resist reaching out and running her hands over the keys. They were, she found, truly noiseless.

"Do you play?" he asked when he woke, turning his tousled head.

"I did for a time," she said, "and was going to take it seriously—" realizing how Englishness had taken over her speech patterns. "But someone told me my hands were too small."

He reached over the coverlet and turned her hands in his. For the third time.

"They are, a little," he said. "But what do you play with, after all? Your hands or your heart?"

I would play with my soul, she thought, if I was sure I had one.

"Which of them do you play with?" she asked him.

"Both," he said. And he took a breath. He shook his head, to dispel what must have been a hangover.

"But most of all, I play with the audience."

He rolled off the bed and pulled a towel round himself. She touched a pale scar beneath his ribcage and he pulled the towel higher.

"I realized when I was younger," he went on. "The difference between a pianist and a performer."

"Which is?"

"Some of my colleagues were better players than me. Infinitely better. But in front of an audience, they froze. Me, I played better."

He held up his hands to the pale light of the window.

"So these hands were playing them."

As they were playing me, she thought, when he asked her to check the time on his ticket to Munich.

It was an 11.30 from nearby Gatwick. She let her head fall back on the pillow while he sidled out the other side and she must have fallen asleep and he must have been as quiet as a ghost or too used to the awkwardness of such situations to attempt to wake her because when she did wake, fully and with a raging, sweating headache, he was gone. She took advantage of the shower, but nothing would dispel that drill behind her eyes. She walked back through the idling seagulls and the whistling wind to the empty garden flat behind the station. She was running a series of alibis through her mind for her bass player, when she remembered he was still a week away in London.

Now she peeled a banana by her kitchen table, gave the peel to the parrot to chew on and wondered which version of herself had ended up here. Her mother died, leaving her the cottage. She had put off visiting it for years, then was enticed westwards with some "crusty" friends for a festival in Schull. She got the keys from the local estate agent and wandered into an unweeded garden, opened the front door to a ruin, smelling of mould and mildew. There were worse things to do than fix it up, she thought, and so began the long round of acquaintances, plumbers, carpenters, roofers, which ended with the banished Peter and herself by the table with the munching parrot. The country had a way of rooting you, she found; life, if not easy, was always possible. You learned to live on a little, and any deviation from that little meant a journey, so you tended to stay. The range of friendships she managed surprised her. Germans, English expatriates, retirees from the media in Dublin and London. And the locals, amongst whom she became known as the "piano lady". She had their children to teach, and spaced out their hours so most of the time was hers. And her past was someone else's, until she saw him by the windy table outside the coffee shop, with his mismatched socks and trainers, and a teacup in his hands.

Those hands that had so carelessly played her. And her own small hands rippled over the laptop now, probing the healing properties of the wells of West Cork. Cures for warts and boils, a whole litany of skin ailments and a remarkable number to do with eyesight. An acolyte whose eyes were so attractive to suitors that she tore them out and could only restore them by bathing the empty sockets in the waters of a well, now long forgotten. So her own little parable, of the reluctant beauty marred by the port-wine blemish, wasn't too far off the mark. It might even play him.

9

She spent the next day writing emails to the mothers of her
ex-pupils and resumed her duties on a Thursday. She found the
front door locked, and walked around to the irregular gardens
at the back. She found him by the semi-circular trellis with a
bucket in one hand and a tangle of rope around his feet.

"A bucket?" she asked him.

"It is a well," he said.

"And every well needs a bucket?"

He managed a brief, embarrassed smile.

"You've given up on the mask?"

"Oh my god—"

And her panic was real. She pulled it from her coat pocket
and was about to slip it on, when he stopped her hand.

"It's alright, you know. We're both in each other's – what's it
called?"

"Bubble?" she ventured.

"Correct. And if you're to work here, we'll have to take our
chances."

She nibbled at her lip. It was the moment. It had come
and gone, without her knowing. And she realized, for some
nights now, she had been visualizing it. The mask slipped, the
recognition in his eyes. My god.

But there was none.

His maskless face turned away to the well and back. She found herself blushing, with anger or embarrassment she couldn't have been sure. Come on, she thought uselessly, tell me you know me.

"You know, it just struck me, I never caught your name."

You have known me. But he smiled, the way the mildest of acquaintances would. And from his point of view, she realized, they were mildly acquainted. The way the queen would have smiled. Politely, with polite interest.

"Tara."

She wondered would that elicit a response. When it didn't, she almost curtsied.

"Tara. William."

He held out his hand again. Formally, this time. The right one.

"We're not meant to shake."

"Of course."

He offered his elbow. She bumped it.

"Your friend's been telling me about the well."

"What about it?"

"The local legend. The saint, with the blemish."

And she had to wonder now. Who was fooling who here?

"She wasn't a saint yet, with the blemish."

"No, of course. The water had to do its work. And the shepherd—"

"Shepherd?"

"The young man who pulled her out. Fell so badly for her... what was his name? Meehawl?"

"It means Michael."

So Peter had come up with a name. How inventive.

"And her name?"

She would have to. Come up with a name.

"Ite," she said. It seemed the simplest.

"He sees her at the fair day, selling the fleece of his prize ram—"

And she had to admire Peter's storytelling now. His elaborations were ridiculous, but impressive.

"He doesn't recognize her."

"Ite? Of course not. But she takes his breath away."

"No good, though, was it?"

"No. She devotes herself to the water. To the well's healing powers. Could be an opera libretto."

"It could be?"

"Yes. He marries. Seven children. Never forgets her. And when his wife dies, old and crabbed, searches her out again."

"He does?"

"Falls into the well. And this time she pulls him out. To find the beautiful youth that had saved her, years ago—"

"Ah. Your Peter didn't get that far. But what a beautiful fancy. To be attached to this rather unlovely hole in the ground."

She walked through the trellis work that Peter had built. It could blow away with the first storm, she realized.

"Did he charge you?"

"Two hundred euro. Plus expenses."

She was selling herself cheap, she knew. Once more.

"And a well needs a bucket?"

"Wouldn't you think?"

He began to tie the rope round the bucket handle.

"But a bucket needs a winch."

"Maybe later."

"There could be no end to the needs of this well."

She took the bucket from his hands and looked at the grassy edge.

"Careful—"

"You're afraid I'll fall in? Come out a dripping, gorgeous thing?"

"In the first flush of your girlhood?"

"You wouldn't recognize me."

And if there was a bait there, he didn't take it.

"I very much fear you wouldn't make it out."

"Hold me then."

She belted her coat and he held it. When she took two steps to the edge, he placed the other hand round her waist. She looked down, remembering the dark waters in Clare and her mother's creaking joints. She dropped the bucket.

She was surprised, and almost shocked, at how the rope burnt through her fingers. The bucket sailed downwards, becoming a diminishing silver orb. The rope whipped on through her palms, and she cried out in pain, had to let it go. And the last yard of rope whipped round her ankle, pulled her closer to the edge and she would have fallen with it, had he not wrapped two hands round her waist to steady her. As it was, she lost her heeled bootee, and watched it falling after the vanishing bucket.

Until they both heard a faraway splash, and he had the presence of mind to clamp his foot on the curling end of the rope.

"Woah."

She was leaning back against him, one of his psoriatic hands on her hip.

"Careful now."

He edged her backwards. He bent down, gripped the rope

with his other hand and began to pull. One hand over the other and the sound of the clunking bucket echoed from below.

"Your hands are bleeding."

"So are yours, my dear."

She looked down and saw that they were.

"I'll need to reinforce it with stone."

"Stone?"

"The surface. Of the well."

"Why?"

"You saw what almost happened."

"What almost happened?"

"You almost fell in."

She could see the bucket approaching. There was something floating in it.

"Give Peter one afternoon with his JCB. He'll have it filled in."

"I wouldn't dream of it."

"Why not?"

"What was her name? The saint?"

"Saint Ite."

"And her well. Filled in by an Englishman?"

"What's wrong with that? You own the place—"

"I don't own the legend."

So that's what it was now. A legend. She wondered was that the way all legends start. A wayward fancy, a well-timed fib. And every haunted house hid a mundane secret, not a ghost. Maybe the Loch Ness monster began with nothing more than a midnight poacher. Dracula was just a necklace fetishist. But. She had to wonder where it came from. Her. And what was the reason for its coming? He had called her dear, she now remembered. And she saw his bleeding hands still pulling at the rope.

They had had some success. The bucket was reaching the rough fringes of the grass. There was something floating in it. Rising up from the dark water the bucket was now filled with. Cleaving off the leather like retreating plastic or barely visible ice. Like a forgotten detail in a fairy tale.

Her shoe.

One of her feet was naked. She could feel the grass, cold, wet and somehow delicious on the skin of her sole.

"We got lucky," he said. He lifted the bucket to where the trellis met the grass and settled it carefully, so as not to spill a drop.

"We did?"

"Your shoe."

It was more of a bootee, really. And it seemed to belong to the last of her former selves. The one that tapped its heel beneath the piano as the local Brighton darlings went through their scales. They had cleaner fingers, were better learners than the Irish ones, she remembered.

"Here—"

He took it out of the bucket and shook it free of drops. He took a handkerchief from his waistcoat pocket and began to wipe it dry, inside and out. He paid particular attention, it seemed to her, to the instep.

What kind of man carries a handkerchief in his waistcoat pocket? A white handkerchief, not covered in engine oil and yellowish stains of forgotten phlegm, with embossed embroidery in one corner. She couldn't read it as he brushed the leather dry, but she could imagine what it spelt. WB.

William Barrow.

"Here," he said, and set it in the grass. "If I may—"

And he took her ankle in his damaged hand.

He settled the shoe on her foot, the way a prince would, she thought, in a fairy tale. An aged prince, with an embossed handkerchief.

And she had to wonder was she wearing the same shoes, that night, so long ago now. She looked down at her feet, the blunt toes of black leather against the dark tangled grass. She decided she couldn't have been.

He was untying the rope from the bucket handle. He looked at the dark water, as it settled.

"It seems blacker, somehow, doesn't it?"

"Blacker?"

"Than ordinary water. Should be."

"Maybe it's been down there for years."

"You think? It's stagnant?"

She dipped her fingers in. Brought it to her nostrils.

"It smells fresh."

"Doesn't all water smell fresh?

"No. Sometimes it smells of nothing. And stagnant water smells of rot."

She brought her fingers to his nostrils.

"What do you think?"

"No rot there. There'd have to be a spring, I suppose."

"Or some underground river."

"Yes. Some kind of constant flow. Well," he said, and looked her in the eye.

He rolled his sleeves up to his elbows.

"Here goes."

He clasped both hands together and dipped them in the bucket.

"It worked for her."

"For who?"

She allowed herself a moment of confusion.

"The blemished beauty."

She saw his fingers clasped together, underneath the water, in a prayerful way.

"What was her name again? The healer?"

She had to think, hard. What was her damn name?

"Ite. And who said she was a healer?"

"You're right. First she was healed."

"You don't believe in this nonsense, do you?"

"Me? A rational Englishman?"

He shook his head.

"Of course not. But."

He withdrew his hands. The water seemed to cleave off them in slow motion. Fingers still intertwined.

"You know what they say. There are no atheists in a foxhole."

"That's a whatdoyoucallit. A metaphor."

"If anything cured me of this, I'd believe it."

She began to establish a regimen inside. She had a tidy, efficient part to herself that began to kick in. Floors, windows, fridge. She found herself done within an hour, and almost disappointed.

"We have to work out a schedule," she told him. He was wrapping gauze around his hands, by the packing cases, and for some reason reminded her of a medieval saint. From some painting by El Greco.

"A schedule?"

She wondered what was underneath the gauze. Some dermatological cream.

"For my hours. Six or seven hours a week, I work it out as. Do you want me one afternoon or two?"

"Two hours a day, perhaps?"

"Ah. That would mean."

She pretended to think. But she knew what it meant. He was lonely.

"I could manage that. I've no more lessons."

"And if you went beyond the hours, of course, I would pay."

Really lonely, she thought. She almost felt sad. And she wondered was she sad for her or him.

"Laundry?" she asked.

It was a delicate subject. For any man.

"I can fill the washer myself."

"Ah. So I'll do the drying?"

"If you'd be so kind."

"Two hours a day then. And I'll make sure to check the dryer."

She made it out the front door and was confused for a moment. She could see no bicycle. She knew it couldn't have been robbed, so walked around the Georgian frontage and saw it parked by the side, near the scullery door. She saw the unruly garden again, the ridiculous trellis and the dark hole that it protected. She walked forward, glancing at the window to check he wasn't there.

She needed a private moment with this well.

It was her own invention, in a way. Her own fancy. Her own weapon. She made it through the trellis and stood there, careful of the crumbling earth. She could hear a low, booming moan, or an echo of a moan, as if some animal had died a long time ago and that cylinder of wet, shining moss retained the memory. She lay down on the grass and inched her body forwards, so her head dangled over the empty space. She felt weightless, floating outside of time, the dark cylinder of green moss falling away below her to the distant lapping of water. She had a secret to tell this thing, whatever it was. I invented a story for you, she told it, but it is no more ridiculous than my own. She heard a boom or a lap that seemed to ask what. So she told it. I know him, she said, who owns the grounds you lie in. I know him and was known by him. Did she say it or just think it? There was a biblical assonance to the thought, know, known, so it felt as if she said it. There was another boom and it was one of those sounds that existed in imagination, as much as it could have in reality. And then she heard, buried somewhere in the low distant boom, the cry of a seagull.

She drew herself back to her feet. She didn't know much about wells. She assumed they originated from some springy source, deep in the earth. But could they possibly be connected to an underground channel that led to a river, that perhaps led to the sea?

She walked back to her bicycle, almost embarrassed. But what could she be embarrassed by? There was nobody looking. And he wasn't the type to hide his gaze, if he did want to look.

She heard the sound again, the low moan and the tiny, scraping cry of what could be a seagull. Was that a memory or imagination? A real sound, or was the well inside her now?

She cycled back down the driveway, feeling embarrassed for her own embarrassment. How could she be so shy about a natural object? Still, when she came to the gates, she turned right, towards the sea, not left towards the town. The road led her to an old dry stone wall, covered in the same green moss. It wasn't wet now, it was shrivelled and almost white, as time had done its job on it. And she could see, running underneath the

73

dry stone wall, and therefore underneath the road, the brownish gleam of running water.

A crevice, with a ripple, far below. She wondered why she'd never heard talk of it before. Still and all, she followed it, lifted her bike over the wall on the opposite side, perched it in the grassy field and followed what she could of the journey of that water. It vanished under old hedges, which she had to negotiate her way around, appeared again underneath a blaze of heather, then vanished again, under huge slabs of limestone. She began to hear a boom then, like the echoing boom of the well itself, and realized it was the sound of waves, crashing against some shore she couldn't see. She came to a sudden cut in the landscape then, and saw that the ocean was close. An explosion of foam came out of the dull, tufted earth. A blowhole, she thought. She had heard of them, and all of the twists of rock surprised her, and beyond them a small drop of cliff and the booming tide.

So the well was fed by an underground stream which made its way to the ocean, here. The oceanic wave, which had the quality of a whisper in the well, became a veritable roar, here. Herring gulls twisting in the spray and gannets, further out, stretching their wings in the curve, readying the dive. It was as if the well had told her one of its secrets. She felt a quiet pleasure, even a power, and determined to keep this secret to herself.

Then she wondered, how could sound travel through a hidden stream? There must be some other outlet. Deep in the bowels of that sheath of wet green moss. And she saw a boat, now, bobbing out beyond the line of surf. A blunt-shouldered figure in yellow slicks, pulling lobster pots.

She recognized Peter. She would have waved, but knew he wouldn't recognize her so far out from the shore. She should get him to reinforce the circle of grass inside the trellis. Some old-fashioned stonework, held together with cement. Then she thought there must be stonework there already. Underneath the grass. It had once surely been a working well.

Who was fooling who, she wondered? William accepted her fancy with all of the politenesss of a well-bred Londoner, but Peter's elaboration on it was another matter entirely. Could they become co-conspirators, she mused, and lead this elderly narcissist down a garden path, which led to a hidden well, which led to a hidden river, which led to a blowhole and the unruly Atlantic beyond? What an exquisite revenge, if revenge was what she was about. She must ask the well, she thought to herself, if revenge was indeed what she was about and, if so, how revenge would play in its story. Before she reminded herself, one more time, that she had invented the whole saga.

10

William Barrow sank into the delicious afternoon comfort of his bed and pillows. This daylight sleeping was a new thing, somehow both refreshing and humiliating. To do with age, of course. He was a diminished thing, but yet, the indulgence of these fifteen or so minutes, which could feel like hours, made it worth it. He wished there was someone he could wake to. Sleep well, dear? The thought brought back the memory of Susannah, and he realized, with that familiar diminishing sense of himself, that he, in truth, was glad that there wasn't. Aloneness was an unfamiliar state, almost like a challenge he had set himself. He would rise to it, if to nothing else. And his sense of isolation was muted by the promise of another visit tomorrow. Five hours a week. One hour a day. He wondered had she seen through the pathetic nature of his request. And he wondered again, before he fell asleep, why he so wanted her here. She seemed already familiar, maybe that was why. But familiarity takes time, and she seemed, somehow, immediately familiar. Maybe something to do with the well, he thought, and his eyes closed.

He awoke, as usual, about ten minutes later. But he could have slept for two hours. He remembered a bearded uncle who would fall asleep in his chair, a spoon between his two fingers, to be woken by the clatter of the same spoon on the wooden floor. So the time it took for the spoon to fall afforded him the length of a rest and time was therefore elastic, not a measurable entity to be beaten out by some invisible metronome. The thought frightened him as a child, because he liked metronomes and the rigour they gave to his practising fingers. The memory reminded him of his bandaged hands and he raised them to the sunlight that poured in through the window and was shocked at what he saw.

The gauze was blemished by patches the colour of old rust. As if the fingers inside them were made of scrap metal, attached with various screws to the two iron plates of his palms. They may as well be, he thought, and began the unwinding of the gauze, delicate and at times painful, as if some biological glue had stuck the material to the skin beneath. And as that skin revealed itself, he saw the old open sores and pustules, bleeding now with the palms and fingers covered in something like brown lichen. So much for a cure, he thought, and he walked downstairs, trailing two banners of soiled gauze behind him. They got caught in the bannisters as he reached the ground floor, and ripped from one hand, then the other, with separate darts of pain, like two electric shocks. He felt the need to speak to her, and would have called her, but realized he didn't have her number. He walked through to the scullery, found some skincare lotion above the fridge, and kneaded both hands with it, hoping for some respite, as he used his hip to push open the scullery door. His hands were useless now, and not only for pressing ivory keys. For turning door handles, opening doors. He made his way into the garden, stood by the new trellis, staring at the dark hole in the ground that it protected. He could hear a distant boom, and something sharp beneath it, like the cry of a bird. He wondered should he blame her, or blame her story of the well. If anything, he should blame that bucket of water he drew from it. Then he wondered was it one of those reactions that presaged a healing, that homeopaths talk about. He was sure the village was full of them. Things get worse, before they get better, kind of supposition. He could have driven to the nearest town, tracked down yet another dermatologist, if he could manage the car keys and the steering wheel with his bleeding hands. But he decided to wait. Until the next morning.

And he was extracting the store-bought lasagne from the oven, both hands wrapped in separate tea towels, when he realized he was waiting for her.

He slept hardly at all that night. He was still awake at four, took a sleeping pill and woke again at ten, to hear the sound of footsteps below him, moving from the boards of the piano room to the flagstones of the scullery. Ka boom, ka boom. Heel and then toe, minim to crotchet. The bleeding, the rust, the lichen, whatever it was had congealed into a second skin on his hands. When he flexed his muscles, the skin cracked. He should be angry, he felt, at her, at the well, at her story of the well, but he felt a strange light-headedness when he closed his eyes to block out the morning sunlight. Maybe it was the sleeping pill. They used opioid substitutes, he had been told, in some of them, which might account for that floating sense of euphoria. He held his useless hands to the sunbeams and thought that the fault was, if anyone's, his alone. He remembered dipping his hands in that bucket. The clasping church steeple of fingers. The strange, almost obscene, childish wish. Make them better.

So he dressed, with difficulty, made his way downstairs and presented them to her.

Proffered. That would have been her word.

"My god," she said, "what happened?"

"The well," he said, "the water."

78

"Water couldn't do that."

"That water did."

"My fault?"

"No. My own."

My fault indeed, she thought, and if revenge was her object, here was the result, two bandaged, bleeding hands once more proffered to her.

She felt he wanted her to hold them. So she did the next best thing. She undid her apron, wrapped it around them and led him, like a child, to the kitchen door.

"The moss," she said.

Why the moss, she wondered? She had heard it somewhere. Hydration. Moss on walls.

"The moss?" he asked.

"It wasn't the water that healed. It was the moss. So the story goes."

And she led him, back through the unruly garden. Inside the trellis, where she knelt by the open hole and reached her hands down to the damp stone beneath. She pulled fistfuls of the wet, green moss and placed it on her skirt, between her spread-out knees. It dampened her skirt, as if she had wet herself, but she didn't care.

"Kneel down," she said and he dutifully knelt. "Here."

She rolled the moss into a paste between her fingers, told him to shake the apron from them, and began to smear it on his hands. Though smear was hardly the word, she thought. It was odd, the way certain words came to suit their situation. Knead.

He proffered his hands. She kneaded the green moss onto their skin.

"The water," she said. "Must have been stagnant after all."

Although, obscurely, she knew it wasn't.

"And moss soaks in bacteria."

"So. She bathed her face in moss, not water."

"Who?"

"The lady of the well."

"Oh. The saint? She must have."

"It definitely provides some relief."

"Good," she said. "We'll do it better inside. More completely."

"Inside. Much better."

Does all affliction lead us to a childhood state, she wondered? It was so easy. One promise of balm to a skin complaint and he became compliant in her hands. She led him back to the kitchen – and led was the word, she held his long, moss-covered fingers in her own, as if he couldn't have made it to the door without her – unrolled fresh strips of gauze on the deal table, covered them in the mossy paste and wrapped his hands once more.

He sat there, while she did the house. He listened to the short and long of her blunt heel and toe on the slate of the kitchen floor, on the wooden boards of the living room, the soft carpet of the ascending stairs. And rather than a musical comparison to that sound, he remembered a rhetorical one. Iambic. One short unstressed syllable followed by a longer one. Susannah, at Glyndebourne, tapping out the rhythms of Britten's *A Midsummer Night's Dream*. She had been a lecturer in English at the polytechnic in Reading when they met. She knew all there was to know about iambs and trochees. He remembered the long flowing skirt and the programme on her lap and their dart underneath the beech trees during the interval when the rain came down. They had missed the second act, to his shame and her delight. They were roughly the same height, which made their coming together seem as natural as the smell of cut grass. I was taller than all the others, she told him in the hotel room that night and it was as surprising to her as to him that the chimera of height sustained their relationship for so long. And now that he remembered, it was the same chimera that endeared them to the empty, draughty house when they first encountered it. Tall ceilings, tall windows, bedroom doors through which neither had to bend their head. Her bare feet padding on the empty floorboards with no particular rhetorical resonance. And he wondered why he was so aware of the sound now. Ka boom, ka boom. If they had happened upon that well, would their future have been different? And the very thought exhausted him, and he realized it wouldn't.

His new housekeeper came into view then, at the foot of the stairs. Small, compact calves and a sinuous way of walking on those heeled sandals. The hair a frizz of blonde around the mask. She was free to take it off now, and he felt that pang again. There must be a reason why she didn't.

"How are they?" she asked and he looked down at his gauzed hands and he realized he hadn't thought of hands, skin or blemishes for what felt like a good hour.

"No difference," he said.

"Give it time," she said.

"Would you like some tea?"

"Let me make it," he said, and pre-empted any objection she could have made by standing, turning to the sink and reaching for the kettle. He had the top off, the water poured and the gas lit before he realized that his fingers had managed all of those tasks without undue discomfort. And as the cloud of steam

81

began to form, he held his gauzed hands above it. The sense of warm condensation was irresistible.

"Do you get lonely on your own?"

It was a question, accompanied by the iambic of her heels across the stone floor.

He shrugged. He knew by the procession of sounds that she was heading towards the kitchen door.

"No visitors?"

"Hardly," he said, "since the business."

"The plague," she said. "Do you mind if I smoke?"

He did, but he didn't want to say it.

"Out here."

"Please don't," he said. "Inside."

"Never inside. Wouldn't dream of it. And I won't here, if you don't want me to?"

"No," he said. "Go ahead. Be my guest."

"OK then."

He heard the flare of a match, as he swirled water in the kettle, dropped in a bag of Barry's tea. And as he poured the steaming water, he could sense the waft of the cigarette smoke, though she was still at the door. One shoulder crooked against the door jamb, one arm with the burning tip angled sideways. The mask dangling round the side of her neck. Her own blue cloud billowing, before the wind took it.

"How are the hands?"

"Somewhat better," he said.

"It's funny," she said, "that English talk."

"What English talk?"

"Somewhat," she said. "I would have just said a bit."

"Tea," he said. "I'll lay yours on the table. I'll take mine upstairs."

"Go ahead," she said.

Be my guest, she thought. And she wondered had she offended him, listening to the procession of his feet towards the stairs, and on up the stairs. Maybe it was the second-hand smoke. She really should get one of those vaping things. She curled the cigarette butt carefully into the stuccoed wall, and dumped the offending object in the waste bag beneath the sink. She saw the tea, sitting there on the deal table and the small milk jug and sugar bowl waiting beside it, and was unaccountably touched. There was a delicacy to the arrangement, the small flowered jug and the chintz bowl, as if a woman had set them.

And she wondered once again why she was doing this. Mary, last afternoon, had asked her the same. She could get the same hourly rate from a piano lesson. It's the cycle, she said, up from the harbour road to the avenue of old trees. It's the fact that I don't have to wipe the piano keys free of sugary hands. And maybe it's the company.

"Company?" Mary had asked. "Don't you have a parrot for that?"

"You know that's almost funny."

The doorbell had tinkled then, a pensioner entered, put an end to their exchange. And Tara had wondered could she ever tell her. Could she ever tell anyone? She could whisper it to Erik the parrot, she supposed. The way the king in that Irish legend had told his secret to an oak tree. Much safer than a parrot, who could learn the words with repetition, but then the oak tree was cut down and fashioned into a harp which sang out his secret anyway. There are no secrets in the end, she knew, somewhere inside herself. They all come out, whether blurted by their guardians, squawked out by a parrot, or echoed out by a harp carved out of an ancient oak.

Then, she obscurely knew where the guardian of her secret was.

The well. It was full of nuance, unexplained depth. It had collapsed beneath him, almost dragged him into its oblivion, could have killed him but had let him live. When she had first looked down into it, she had breathed her secret into it and now it held it, like an undead thing, waiting for its moment. So the fantasia she had come up with about it was just a diversion. A long suspended chord, for the cacophony to come.

But she drank her tea by the deal table, and couldn't explain to herself why this long suspension was such a divertissement, to keep the musical metaphors going, such a delicious elongation of a necessary, expected, even inevitable moment. When he would look at her, strike his forehead with his damaged hands and go—

Of course.

The recognition. Was that what she was waiting for, being paid for by the hour? Perhaps. The flood of memory, the embarrassment, the blush, if that veined face of his could ever blush. If so, she realized she didn't want it yet. The waiting was the prelude. Or the andante. Whatever came before the big finale.

She walked outside, dragged her way through the undergrowth to where Peter's improvised trellis circled the grassy hole. She lay down her mug outside the perimeter and began pulling at the grass. It came away in clumps, as if hair had been combed over to cover an ancient, balding pate. And she felt the damp of old stone beneath it. She got a trowel from the garden shed and an ancient clipper and began to scour and cut. And there it was, a semi-circle of old stone that the grass had hidden. Peter's trellis marked it almost perfectly, and the circle of the well she could now see was more of an oval, like an open mouth. She had allowed it into her secrets, and she wondered would the well someday return the favour.

A winch, she thought. She must ask Peter to get a winch for the rope and bucket.

11

He woke the next morning, alone as usual. There was the sound
of a breeze rattling the windows and as he dressed he watched
the tips of the avenue trees do their trembling dance. There were
leaves curling in the air like colourless confetti and he thought
he knew what kind of day it was. He raised his hands to the
daylight and was mildly surprised by the gauze wrapping that
covered them. Then he remembered. The churning of the moss
in her apron, her green-smeared hands on his own, the wrapping
afterwards. There was a well, of course. Some story about it. The
gauze had turned a uniform green, as if the hands beneath were
made of copper that had oxidized. He moved into the bathroom
and began to manipulate his toothbrush with his green wrapped
hands, thought of tearing the gauze off, and then decided against
it. He could uncurl them, though, which was at least unusual. He
could make toast, down in the kitchen, butter it, fill the kettle,
make a pot of tea, all without thinking about the effects on his
damaged skin. Perhaps it was simply the gauze wrapping, which
placed it out of sight and therefore out of mind.

He decided to take a drive. His leather gloves sat on the
passenger seat of the ancient Jaguar, as if daring him to attempt
to put them on. But with his wrapped hands, there was no
need. The engine coughed to life, and as he edged the car

forwards, the wheel slipped easily between his fingers. He drove through the village, towards the town of Bantry, then turned down one of those side roads that led to one of the many fjords this part of the country was blessed with. The kinds of hidden treasures that attracted retired London journalists, barristers, spread like a secret code between them. Jeremy Morton had been one of the first, retired from the BBC, so long there that he looked with a kind of disdain on each new arrival. He had always meant to call, announce his permanent presence there and for some private reason never did. Silence was hard to explain. The hands were the issue and the less said about them the better. And as he pulled into the forecourt, a gravelled driveway that led to a restored farm or mill house, sitting just above an expanse of sea or river, he realized an unannounced arrival might not be welcome.

The windows were shuttered and he knocked uselessly on the door for a minute or two. Then he walked round the back and saw the field of grass, curving down towards the river, if river it was, where an old swing hung from a sycamore tree. He made his way down towards it and sat on the swing, almost daring the two old strands of rope above it to take his weight. There was the groan from the branch above and the faint creak of a tightening knot, but nothing gave way. So he began to swing, idly, and almost tumbled backwards, grabbed the rope with both of his bandaged hands. There was a simple pleasure to the motion then that he gave himself to. The sheen of silver water began to rise and fall in his vision, and a gannet plunged suddenly downwards and hit the water, which he decided was the sea, not a river. So it couldn't have been a mill house. Some early Victorian farm, by an inlet, restored with a BBC pension. He must have had children, Jeremy, hence the swing. And he, William Barrow, realized how little he knew about Jeremy Morton. How little, indeed, he knew about himself. It was a childhood sensation, this gentle rocking backwards and forwards, but one that he couldn't recall from any childhood of his own. And he began to wonder had he ever had one, that period of bliss that the books and the memoirs described. He had been a child once, could remember the chafing of the short pants against his skin, but he could not, for the life of him, remember a swing. Couldn't remember the movement of children's shoes against a swinging landscape, like his own trainers now, cleaving through that expanse of water into the sky, and as the sky suddenly tumbled and seemed to whirl above him, he felt a sharp jolt of pain as his shoulder hit the grass. He had fallen. He allowed himself to roll, towards the water below, and rolled to a standstill, staring at the scudding clouds above. A few errant leaves blew below them and as he watched them circle downwards, he wondered would he ever be able to rise. He had collapsed, a man in his early seventies, with greying hair and damaged hands, and there was no-one to help him up. No-one to observe, no-one to know that he had fallen. He could feel his thumping heart, and he wondered, if he had expired there, with the swing still arcing behind him, would it even be a death. If a tree falls in the forest and there's no-one to hear it, does it make a sound? He turned then, placed both bandaged palms on the grass, and felt the ache in his shoulder as he forced himself to rise. He walked back towards the empty house, towards his car, realizing that he hadn't died, but that he would, one day. And that he didn't want a death unobserved.

He parked beside the coffee shop on his way back. What did he want? Nothing, really. Some herbal tea, maybe, a punnet of black olives. But whatever he wanted was a subterfuge. What he really wanted was to see was she there.

"I can take that announcement down now?" Mary asked, wrapping the unnecessary olives. "Don't want to be flooded with candidates."

"Of course," he said and walked to the noticeboard, tore it down and crumpled it. Then he realized the implications of her statement. It was a small town, after all. The smallest. For some reason, he blushed.

"She was in here earlier."

"Who?"

"Tara."

"Of course, Tara."

Of course, that was her name.

"Cycled on up to your place. She has her own key?"

"No," he said, "she doesn't."

He ordered two wraps then, chicken and pesto. Why two, he wondered? He must be hungry.

"She'll be kicking her heels outside, then."

"How remiss of me."

"Remiss," Mary said, handing him his change. "Nice word."

So he drove up the avenue, saw her bike, perched by the pillar. The red plastic raincoat curled over the handlebars. He placed the key in the lock, opened the door and saw her shadow through the back window, out in the field behind.

He left the door open and turned right, walked past the haphazard window to the rear of the house and found her, wiping the glass with the palm of her hand.

"Would you like a sandwich?" he asked.

"A sandwich?" she asked.

"Sorry," he said. "What is it called? A wrap."

88

"Love one," she said.

"Where should we have it?"

"Try that patch of grass, down there."

She pointed. Then she walked. A small semi-circle of green, amongst the dandelions and nettles.

"You need to get them cleaned," she said. "The windows."

"I do?"

He handed her one wrap. Then unwrapped his own.

"I could arrange it for you."

"Your friend Peter?"

"No," she said. "We've had enough of Peter."

She sank to the grass in one simple movement. He tried the same, but couldn't manage it. He had to kneel, splay one leg outwards, support himself with a hand against the grass. Then sit.

"You OK?"

"Yes," he said. He wanted to keep his damaged shoulder to himself. Old age. What was one simple movement becomes three.

"I feel," she said, as she unwrapped her parcel of food, "as if I'm sitting somewhere off, looking onto us both. Like that painting, of the girl in the American field, looking at the house."

"Andrew Wyeth?" he asked.

"Whatever his name was. Hers was Christina."

"But she was on her own."

"Yes," she said. "And there's two of us. Work it out."

"Work what out?"

"I don't know. Whatever. Why I feel like that."

She had eaten only half of her wrap. Lifted the corners of the paper back around it.

"You're not hungry?"

"Not that," she said. "I'm here to work."

She moved back towards the house, and then turned.

"You going to sleep?"

"Sleep?"

"You often seem to, at this hour."

"What hour is it?"

"Two. Just after. And if you want to," she said, "I'll keep it quiet."

He finished his wrap, watching her walk towards the house. He wondered how much he had revealed of himself. That he often did sleep at this hour. What hour was it? He turned his green bandaged hand to expose his wrist and looked at his watch. Half two. And the languorous sound of a bumblebee floated past him and he suddenly felt tired. She was right.

Would she always be right, he wondered? He entered the front door and saw her dusting the piano. He resisted the urge to flex his bound fingers on the keys.

"You must remind me," he said. "To get you a key cut."

"So I won't be waiting outside?"

"Apologies," he said.

"You don't have a spare?"

"No."

"Well then. I'll remind you."

She rubbed the dustcloth down the piano keys and he heard a succession of sounds that could have come from some modernist or other. Ligeti, maybe. And as he moved past her, and up the staircase, he for some reason began thinking of the well.

He entered his bedroom and was drawn to the left-hand window. There was a blaze of green through the bubbled glass. The sun threw the shadows of the half-built trellis on the brilliant grass and he realized how the colour green had always soothed him. *Verde que te quiero verde.* A poem by someone in a language he hardly knew. Spanish. Lorca. The shadows seemed to be stretching their long fingers towards the darker hole of the well. An entry of some kind into a shadowed world. Omphalos. Women had always served that purpose in his life. A point of entry into... what? Another version of himself, perhaps. Better or worse, he could never be sure. He stepped backwards towards the bed, felt the mattress touch his calves and stretched down onto it without looking behind. A delicious languor took him over and he raised his hands into the dancing light that played below the ceiling. He felt like touching himself and would have, but for those gauze wrappings. He was so far beyond any kind of desire these days that even the instinct was a surprise. Foreign to him now, like a forgotten lover. And as he closed his eyes, a green membrane seemed to flit beneath his eyelids before the darkness descended.

He awoke ten minutes later, feeling once again as if he'd slept for hours. Something was worrying his cheek. His hand, he realized. Something else was burrowing beneath the zip of his trousers. His other hand. He pulled it back, as if stung with some obscure guilt, and saw, to his amazement, that it was gauzeless. The threads of green-stained bandage wound about the coverlet like elongated flags. And his hands were the colour of lime or lichen, as if he had dipped them in a bowl of zest. The skin was supple beneath it, or if not yet smooth, more untroubled than it had been for years.

He brushed his cheeks with his palms, and felt the stubble there. He needed to shave, he remembered, but with it came the memory of the unpleasantness of flowing water on those fingers, the stinging pain of soap. He turned his palm and brushed the same stubbled cheek with the back of his fingers. They felt smooth for once, smooth and unlesioned. He rolled out of the bed and padded towards the bathroom. He saw the plastic razor there, barely used, beside the soap and the shaving brush. He turned the tap and hardly dared to place his hand beneath it. But he decided to dare then, and watched as the warm water paled the lichen green of his fingers. He took the shaving brush in one hand, the soap in the other, and pestled it into a foam, which he spread on his cheeks. And it was odd, he realized, as he shaved, how reassuring such a once-simple action could be. The skin of his hands didn't resist, didn't ache, didn't sting. He dipped a towel in the hot flowing water and wiped the foam off his shaven face. And was the sunlight playing tricks with his eyes, or was there a patina of copper green beneath the glass of the mirror? Whatever it was, for a moment or two, he was looking at himself anew, a lichen-coloured lime-green man. Then he rubbed his face and the illusion vanished.

It was simpler than that. He had managed to shave, methodically, calmly, completely.

He walked downstairs, flexing his newborn fingers. He wondered would he surprise her with his own surprise. And to his immense disappointment, when he descended, he saw and then heard, through the silence, that she was no longer there.

He sat by the creaking piano stool. He felt the untroubled skin of his fingers, stretched them again. Then he brought them, almost trembling, to the keys and began to play.

She was carrying a plastic rubbish bag to the bin around the back. When she heard it first, she thought it was a record. Rachmaninoff, *Rhapsody on a Theme of Paganini*. But played by whom? Could he possibly be listening to his own recordings? Then a huge, sonorous chord was held, as if to listen to itself, and she knew it couldn't be. He was actually, physically playing. She raised the bin lid tentatively, as if not to disturb the sound. She let the bag fall in like a soughing ghost. She replaced the lid. She had her red coat wrapped round her shoulders. The bin delivery was the last of her jobs. She walked around the back of the house, past the old cramped window which led to corridors she would one day clean, and came to the large Georgian window that looked sideways into the living room.

He was for some reason playing, his long form bent over the piano keys, his fingers rippling across them in that way she now realized she would always remember, in the Wigmore Hall, in the Brighton Dome. He was wearing an old, collarless grandfather shirt, the sleeves dangling round his elbows, and his hands were unbound. Instead of an elegant dress-suit with a bow tie. The feet that pressed the pedals were clad in trainers. She stood, listening, and knew, somehow, he wouldn't turn around. It was as if nothing else existed, least of all her. She remembered that feeling. She could have quenched it by knocking on the window, shattering the glass with a stone, killing that beautiful, terrible sound, but she knew she never would. She wouldn't even worry the front door. She would angle her bike from the portico pillar, walk it quietly down the avenue towards the trees, and only when she was certain that squeaking wheels would not disturb him would she mount the saddle and cycle towards home.

This she did, so the music gradually receded from her, to be replaced by the sound of her squeaking bicycle. It was like a disappearing memory, too beautiful, too terrible to live in. She must give up this job, she felt. Rachmaninoff, she remembered her theory teacher telling her, had turned Paganini's melody for the violin backwards, an idea she never fully understood. But the more distant the sound became now, the more backwards it seemed.

12

It was ridiculous, she thought as her cottage came into view. She had to tell him. Or she had to tell someone, other than that sliver of water at the bottom of that mossy drop. It would end in chaos otherwise. Tell him or stop the cycle down the avenue; the floors were all scrubbed anyway. The work consisted of nothing more than messages and tidying. It would end in damage, somebody's death, hers or his. She imagined an argument, one of the knives from the butcher's block sliced across somebody's throat. Hers, but most probably his. But did he deserve that kind of punishment for what was only an excess of narcissism, an abundance of everything she lacked in terms of self-regard? A narcissistic celebrity, who forgot most of those who crossed his path. Was that an actionable crime? In her terms, maybe, but hardly in anyone else's.

So she passed her own gate and for some reason the bike's momentum and that mysterious thing called gravity carried her down to the harbour. She could hear the put-put of a motor and when the harbour came into view behind the thin line of sally trees, she knew it wasn't only gravity that had drawn her there. It was Peter's boat.

He had tied it to the rusted rings and was shaking out the nets and lines in that random way that fishermen do. Herself, she would have threaded each line carefully, separated one from the other, but he just shook, with a logic in the process that untangled them in some mysterious way.

"Tara," he said, and didn't take his eyes from her knees as she got off the bike.

"Peter."

"Is it about that well of yours?"

"Well," she said. "It is and it isn't. Let's have a drink."

"When I've cleaned up here."

"I'll wait for you up in Mac's?"

"OK," he said.

The cure for isolation was at hand, she knew, as she pushed the bike back up the hill. For some reason she didn't want to attempt the cycle. A pint or two and a pizza, and he'd be suggesting some weary stagger back to hers. Could they not just be friends, she would say, knowing the hand would drop on her hip from behind. Friends indeed.

She ordered a Guinness for him and a Chardonnay for herself, took them both outside and hoped his arrival would time itself with the settling pint. And it did, for once, and his gratitude was obvious.

"I saw you," he said, "from the boat, behind an explosion of surf."

"Sounds romantic," she said.

"The blowhole," he said. "Were you checking on my boat?"

"No," she said, "I was following an underground stream."

"There is one?"

"Sounded like it. From the well."

"A well comes from a spring."

"Not always."

"So what is it?" he asked. "The stream of Saint Whatshername?

Ite? She had to make water, felt the pressure on her bladder, raised her skirts and let go. And her waters flowed from there to the blowhole. And the river was called—"

"Don't laugh," said Tara.

"I'm trying not to," he said. "Just wondering what the hell you're up to."

"I know him," she said. And she immediately wished she hadn't.

"Who? The piano geezer?"

"Yes."

"You're cleaning for him. Of course you know him."

"That's not it," she said. "I know him from before."

"Aha."

He lengthened both vowels, then blew on the froth of his pint.

"Know him how?"

"He judged a competition I was in when I was fifteen. Saw him again at a concert in London. At another one in Brighton."

"So? He's happy to have you back. Old acquaintance—"

"No. The thing is, he never remembers. One time from the other. So I could have been a different person."

"Well, maybe you were."

She took a sip of the warm wine. She thought of asking for a colder one, then decided it was hardly worth it.

"If you met me, in fifteen years' time, would you know me?"

"If you'd let me," he said, and brushed his finger off hers across the bench top.

"That wasn't the question. Not would you acknowledge me. Would you want something off me. Would you remember?"

"How could I forget?"

"It's all gone arseways anyhow."

"What has?"

"The questions."

"What's bugging you, Tara?"

"I'm afraid, I suppose."

"Afraid of what?"

"That I haven't invented anything. That it's all true."

"You mean you didn't make it up?"

"Can't tell any more."

She took another sip. It felt vinegary now, more than warm. She was past caring.

"I trawled the Internet," he said. "There was no holy well around here."

"Well," she said, and downed the last of her vinegar. "There is now. And we need a winch, to draw the bucket up."

"He'll pay me?"

"Oh yes. He'll pay alright."

She walked home. She entered her own door, knowing he would follow. She was feeding the parrot a sliver of banana skin when she heard his knock. She had sought him out after all, and it seemed only polite to admit him. At least that's what she told him, when she felt his fishy arms around her neck, allowed a small flurry of kisses and showed him the door.

"It's done, Peter," she told him. "Over."

For his own part, though, it wasn't done at all. He turned left outside her house, instead of right towards the harbour, and after an hour or so of staggering under the moonlight, found himself outside the rectory. He could hear music. The sound seemed borne on the low, mean wind that blew between the hedges. It drew him to the rectory gates, cascades of arpeggios that stopped and started, like surf against distant rocks. He followed the sound then, down the avenue, through the trees and across the lawn, where he could see a figure, bent beside the piano, through the mottled window. It seemed smaller than the English gent, more crabbed somehow, then, as the flurry of notes ascended and the body seemed to take an inward breath, somehow taller, like a shadow elongated by a low footlight. He had stayed too late in the pub, the walk hadn't cleared his head yet. And yet. And yet.

She had said something about a winch. He could see the trellis he had made around the well across the uncut lawns. He should take a measurement, in the moonlight. For some reason that phrase made him giggle. The music surged, and he laughed out loud. He felt the mad urge to dance. Was it him or his shoes felt it? He couldn't be sure. But in that ecstasy of isolation, when one is certain one is unobserved, it didn't seem to matter. He drew one foot in a semi-circle across the leaf-scattered grass. The knee behind it bent and his head arced back, the tendons of his neck stretched almost to bursting point. Two arms shot heavenwards and the knee jerked straight. He managed a twirl then, and collapsed in wheezing laughter amongst the autumn leaves.

He allowed his cheek to fall back against the grasses, and then saw it.

Huge ears, pointing towards the moon, which threw its own shadow. Fore feet perched like a kangaroo, eyes like saucers, staring at his.

A hare.

It seemed to know what it was about. Shivered once, in the moonlight, then turned and darted towards the well.

It left the trellis he had built around it shaking. Bounded once and was gone, into the dark circle beyond.

He shook his head to dispel the drink, hardly sure of what he had seen. But the trellis was still shaking.

And a wind blew up from the ocean side to shake it more.

He rose, walked towards the trellis and stilled it with his hand.

Stared into the dark waters below, expecting to see a ripple there.

But there was nothing. And the music had gone.

13

Over the next week, she waited. For what, she wasn't sure. For that piece of absurd fantasy to retreat, for the stain of green to fade from his fingers, to be replaced by the flaking, broken scars of reddened skin. He would come to her with whatever sad lunch he had prepared – and he always, for some reason, prepared something, perhaps a culinary request would have been too much of an intimacy. A piece of microwaved quiche, from Mary Culleton's, where else, with maybe a sprinkling of salad or coleslaw from the SuperValu. Anyway, he would come to her, a roll of unwrapped gauze in his hands, and say, shall we?

She would lead him out then, always her in front, kneel inside the already unsteady fencing where Peter had somehow erected a winch set in two blocks of concrete and pull handfuls of damp moss from the circular stones below and dump them onto a tea towel. She would knead them with her own hands and take a breath before he proffered his. Always the same, the kneading before the proffering. Then run her green-smeared hands over his, always marvelling at how long the fingers were.

Small hands, he said, on the fifth day, or was it the sixth?

Anyway, it was at the end of a long week, which seemed almost purple with waiting. Purple, where did that word come from? Pregnant, she would have thought, if she were to describe the feeling, but purple was what it felt like. Like a child's face, before it cried, though what would she know of a child's face, like a male lover's thing, before the business began.

She knew it would happen, despite the presence of the mask, and she knew, obscurely, that he knew it too. So on the fifth day, or was it the sixth, when she was kneeling by the imaginary well, the tea towel across her knees full of green kneaded slime, and he was holding his hands in the April sun, waiting for the paste to dry, something rustled in the field behind her.

"Don't move," he said, "it's magical."

"What?" she asked, and almost turned. But he stopped her with one hand to her cheek.

"A hare. Look carefully."

And he pushed her cheek gently, anti-clockwise. So she turned, without even a rustle of movement, and saw it.

Two ears, stretching up, brown against the dandelion yellow. Two eyes, staring directly towards her, though they were so far away she could not so much see them as feel them.

And then the same hand against her cheek, dusty with the dried green moss, lifted her mask and she knew the kiss was coming. She stared towards where the hare's eyes should have been, saw the ears tremble in anticipation, then saw it dart through the dandelions. Then she turned, to meet his kiss.

She was surprised at how supple his lips felt, after all of those years. And surprised at how right something felt. Although it shouldn't have felt right at all.

Everything else was ancillary to the kiss. She remembered movies, when sex seriously entered into them, in the early seventies, and wondered did all of the other stuff, the fumbling with the clothes, the grasping hands, the opened panting mouths, the buttocks of the male or the female heaving beneath whatever surface the principals found themselves on, really have to happen. Oliver Reed in *Women in Love*, Julie Christie in *Don't Look Now*. She knew they had to put their clothes back on after the thing, but was it so important, the before or after? And please, please don't ever ask her about *I Am Curious (Yellow)*. The kiss was the thing, it was always the thing, in the Astor or the Electric or whatever sullen flea pit she used to frequent, as it was now, and the rest was the afterthought. The raising of the dress, the fumbling with the belt, but with one significant difference here. Their surface was the stone, overlaid with fading cut grass, bound by the fencing that Peter had erected and, more than the grass, the tea towel she had spread out over it with its own surface of pulpy, moist, already kneaded moss. It spread on her buttocks, then on his, on her calves, then on his, on her hands, as she smeared them down his blessedly thin stomach to facilitate his entry into her for the second time. She wondered was the hare still peeping from somewhere beyond the dandelions and realized she didn't care if the hare was looking with all of his clutch, but a clutch was the collective noun for chickens she realized, what was it for hares and so she asked him.

"What is for hares?" she asked him.

He laughed at the absurdity of it.

"What is what for hares?"

"The whatdoyoucallit it. Collective noun."

"A husk," he said.

"Ah," she replied. "You would know things like that."

"I would," he said, "being English."

"A husk of hares. What if they're watching?"

"If they are," he said, "they'll keep it secret."

So she had her secret, the well had its secret, and now they had their secret.

"Will you," she asked him, "keep this secret?"

"If you want me to."

"I very much do," she said.

"Then I will," he said, and stroked her cheek with his green fingers. And she wondered again when would the recognition come and realized that, for the moment at least, she didn't care.

Her habits didn't change after that, but they became just that. Habits. The cycle five times weekly to the rectory, the visit to the supermarket in between, a drink with Peter on the Friday or the Saturday and the almost ritual refusal to let him inside her front door.

"People are talking," Mary Culleton let drop to her, while the froth on her cappuccino bubbled away.

"Talking?" she repeated, and already felt the blush spreading upwards. Why upwards, she wondered, idly, as if to prevent its rise. From the heart, she imagined.

"About the rectory," Mary said.

"What about the rectory?" she asked, almost as repetitive as her own parrot. She had known something would come out someday; she had imagined Peter would be the reason for whatever rumours would circulate about her, and she had already prepared her dismissive denial.

"That well," Mary said.

"Well," she repeated. And even the sound of the word came as a relief to her. She could picture the dark green cylinder, falling away from her gaze, and for that moment at least, it felt like a saviour.

★

She had been wondering how long it would take for her habits to be noticed. The ritual punctuality of her cycle down that avenue, the waves of arpeggios as she turned the key in the door, the dance her heels made across the wooden floor and the flagstones, his tinkling on the piano almost making it a ballet. The moment would arrive and they both knew it would arrive, but neither of them knew when or where. The playing would stop and he would come behind her in the kitchen, or it would stop when she would shift his feet with the straw broom. Whenever or however it happened, the playing would stop, he would set aside the prickly broom, which it amused him to call her witch's brush, or she would back into him while opening the fridge and it would be happening again. It amused him to think of them as teenagers, his groans when he had to bend down towards her and his knees would crack, or her pleas to save her the damage to her spine of the flagstone floor, and his riposte that he wished he had the strength and would carry her upstairs if he could. Anyway, however or wherever it happened, it would happen, sometimes even on the bed upstairs, and it would generally end with his whimsical exhale of breath, and he would say, for the seventh or the eighth time or the nineteenth time, I am definitely too old for this.

"Me too," she would reply. And then would come his ritual objection.

"Not at all."

Or sometimes it was, "Please, darling, not at all."

And maybe she wasn't. But if she wasn't, she must be growing younger. She had always been, if not a smart dresser, at least a vogueish one. The red hooded raincoat, the chunky heels, the short pleated skirts she retained from her club-going days, so she didn't have to change her style to dress the way she felt. But she felt something had to show, something in the way she moved, as the song said, or the way she tossed her hair, the way she avoided Mary Culleton's glance, when she cranked the coffee handle, said no sugar, no chocolate?

So she had assumed, someday, she would hear that phrase, people are talking. And she had prepared a litany of responses, from denial to indifference. And to hear the well become the source of gossip was a kind of blessing in disguise.

What else can this well give me, she wondered? But what she said was:

"The well?"

"That well his lordship almost fell into. That Peter had to build a fence around."

"And a winch," she added. "So what about it?"

"Some fucking story, legend, whatever they call it."

"Peter told you that?"

"Who else?" Mary continued, offering up the mug of coffee, and Tara had to touch her hand to prevent the automatic sprinkling of the chocolate.

"Sorry. No chocolate, no sugar. And yes, Peter told me. I thought all that crap was over and done with. We've enough nonsense in the vicinity, without bringing sacred springs into it."

"Sacred springs?"

"Or holy wells."

"Who said holy?"

"The same Peter. Something about a legend. A saint with a scar."

"Not a scar, a blemish."

"So. He did get it from you."

"Not from me. From the legend."

"And how did you hear it?"

"From the piano man himself," she lied. And she could feel the blush returning.

"Where did he hear it?"

"Search me."

"He's the kind of gullible Englishman that would believe anything."

"Are the English gullible?"

"It's a kind of shame with them. They have to believe. Or pretend to believe. Whatever nonsense we feed them."

"He has a great-aunt from here. Way back."

"So. He should know better."

"What if it isn't nonsense, Mary?"

"What isn't nonsense?"

"The story."

"Tell me, then."

It was a strange relief to recount it, and as she did, she began to understand something about stories. Legends, designed to disguise reality. It was as if the well had arranged itself to hide her embarrassment. So she told, about Ite, with the blemished face, not a saint yet, gazing in the waters at her own face, and she added some embellishments here, a father, ashamed of an unmarriageable daughter, the daughter surprised by the goatherd, falling in, being rescued, seen the next week at market, unrecognizable and marriageable at last. It was a good story, she had to admit.

"And what then? "Mary asked.

"She devotes herself to the well. Loses all interest in—"

"In what?"

"What do you think, Mary? Marriage, fornication, children, the whole deal."

"My god," Mary said. "You're going to tell me next that where she made water roses grew."

"Who knows, maybe they did. But that's not the thing, Mary."

"No?"

"No. There's something older there."

"There is?"

"Maybe the story hides another story. The legend hides something much older that has to be hidden."

"What has to be hidden?"

"That's the question."

"You're trying to spook me, Tara."

"Maybe. And if so, I'm spooking myself."

It was odd, she thought. She had all of Mary's attention now, who hardly noticed the several rings on the door, as people came and went. And she could elaborate for hours on this story, this well, all to hide the other hints that she felt her friend was bound, someday, to notice. That she was shagging this old pianist in his rectory, with the enthusiasm of her teenage self.

"What do you know about hares?"

"I've had a hare stew."

"Yeah, but what about them?"

"Hares? They say they dance, in the moonlight."

"Have you ever seen that?"

"No. It's a whatsitcalled. An old wives' tale."

"I must be an old wife then."

"You never married, Tara, unless there's something you're not telling me."

"There is."

"So, tell me."

"I've seen hares, round that well."

"In the moonlight? Dancing?"

"Kind of spooky."

"How spooky?"

"Because there's something in the water. Or the moss around the walls that does things."

"What things?"

"Healing things. His hands. You must have seen them."

"I did. Blisters, pitiful."

"No more pitiful. He can play again."

"Music while you work. Must help pass the time."

"It does."

"Sounds nice."

"It is."

And she took her cappuccino outside, feeling she had said too much already.

She could feel the gaze from inside on the back of her blushing neck as she sat there, in the light spring breeze, blowing the hot froth of the cup to cool it. Is there something inside all of us, she wondered, that wants to tell? It must make it easy then, the interrogator's job, behind the two-way mirror, with whatever criminal turned up in the latest episode of whatever cop show turned up on TV. Just ask innocuous question after question and wait, he, or less often she, will eventually unburden themselves. She had let Mary in on something, she was too well aware, something that would come out sometime, so why not unburden herself and come right out with it? Because, she realized, she was many people. The one these shops, that pub, that supermarket knew was not the one who woke, morning sick and retching, in the basement flat in Brighton. Was not the one who planned a desultory but exquisite revenge, as she cycled down the avenue of elm and poplar trees.

Whatever happened to revenge, she wondered, as she laid

down her half-drunk cappuccino, and for once didn't return the cup and saucer to Mary's counter back inside. Life, just like the story, was full of surprises.

She could always tell the parrot. His attempts at Satie were stillborn anyway, he never got past the first four bars. And she couldn't imagine a better interrogator than him, if indeed it was a him. The eye would stare at her, waiting for the next revelation, the beak opening and closing with its crunching click. There was a girl, she would tell him, whose hands were too small and thus received just a special mention in the Feis Ceoil, who met the same pianist twice again until he turned up, all spent and wasted, in a village in West Cork. And there was one other thing, if this was indeed the interrogation, that would yet come out.

But life, she found, was the best interrogator of all. And happiness becomes itself a kind of torture. So eventually, she let it slip.

14

Their habit had become just that, a habit, and like any habit, it demanded comfort. So what had begun by the piano, on the sofa, on the flagstones beneath the stuttering fridge, resolved itself on the smoother covers of the four-poster bed upstairs. He had come in from the shower, wrapping himself in the robe that he always left hanging there when she curled towards him, beneath the duvet. She needed cover lately, she had lost that naked self-abandon years ago. She turned towards him, her eyes heavy with sleep and sex, and touched the fabric. Silk. Embossed. WB.

"Play me something."

"What?"

There was rain on the windows.

"That Debussy thing. About gardens in the rain."

"*Jardins Sous La Pluie.*"

He stood up, in a rustle of silk. Of course, she thought. His French would be perfect, too. She heard his feet pad down the stairway. Heard the piano lid open. And the first few chords she could never forget.

"Not Debussy," she heard. "But it suits the rain. Shostakovich. *Preludes and Fugues.*"

She dressed, listening. Put on her shoes. Made her way downstairs.

"Is it possible?" he asked, still playing. "That I could manage these, finally? I could never really release them from the stranglehold of Bach."

"Yes, I know," she said.

"You know? You've heard these before?"

"On a record, maybe."

"I've never recorded it."

And his fingers stopped.

"Is there something you're not telling me?"

And Tara had to take a breath.

"Maybe."

"Another legend?"

"No. This one's true."

Now it was his turn. She heard the huge inhale. As if an invisible nail had pierced the sole of his foot. Then the slow exhale.

"You had better say it, then."

She didn't want to, but now knew she had to. She couldn't look at him, and she had to tell him why. As if under the gaze of an unseen interrogator, with an eye as inescapable as that of her parrot. She had always known it would happen, sooner or later, when the sex thing ended, and the sex thing always ends. She realized around the same time that she was never sure about this sex thing anyway. It's a young girl's game, she thought. All of that fumbling with the clothes, all of that blood to the head.

"I heard it," she said, "on April 21st, 1986, in that Grand Hotel in Brighton."

He rubbed one hand over the other. Softly, as if afraid the affliction would come back.

"When?" he asked.

And she repeated it.

"And we—"

"Yes," she said.

"Did I wear the same robe?"

"Probably."

"I should have realized."

"Well," she said. "I knew. Immediately."

"When?" he asked again.

"When I saw you, sitting with your herbal tea. Outside Mary's caff. With your trainers and your mismatched socks. I thought, how could he?"

"How could he what?"

"Dress like that."

"Brighton?" he asked.

"I went to hear you in the Brighton Dome. You played Shostakovich's second concerto and those preludes and fugues. Badly, I thought. We met, at the reception in the foyer. Went back to your hotel room. And with that boundless narcissism that has walked you through your life, you forgot all about it."

"I should have known."

"How?"

"When I saw you cycling up. That red hooded thing. It reminded me of something."

"Of what?"

"Just a feeling."

"Little Red Riding Hood. And you're going to hate me now."

"So that was why the mask?"

"No. The mask was for your protection. Under the NPHET guidelines."

He began to breathe fast, shortly and shallowly.

"You still haven't told me why."

"Why what?"

"Why the whole thing?"

"I could say the same. You never told me why."

"Why what?"

"Why never a phone call."

"Did you give me your number?"

"You know, I forget."

"So it was just one night?"

"There were others."

"I don't believe this—"

"Not like that one."

His hand was trembling, now, by the piano. She took one step towards him and touched it. And it maddened her that, after all of it, she still felt the need to comfort. The lesions would begin again.

"You judged a piano competition, in the Father Matthew Hall, North Circular Road."

"Where?"

"Dublin. You found me wanting then too."

Though that was unfair, she thought to herself. He had not been unkind.

"I did?"

"You gave me special mention. But said my hands were small."

And he looked down at her hand now, lying on his.

"They are, a little—"

"You said the same in the Wigmore Hall."

"London?"

"Yes."

"Where we—?"

"No. We drank champagne and left it at that."

"So you've been following me?"

"Actually, it could well have been you following me."

"How?"

"Think about it. I live here. You kind of turned up."

"And Brighton?"

"Again, I lived there. You kind of—"

She had to smile.

"Turned up. On the poster, on the promenade. William Barrow, an evening at the Dome."

"But you went along."

"Yes. I bought a ticket. Wild horses wouldn't have stopped me."

"And then?"

"Nothing. Till I saw you again in Mary Culleton's."

Was this easy? She couldn't be sure. It would end in something like hatred, she was sure of that.

"And why didn't you say?"

"When I took the job?"

She shrugged.

"It would have seemed kind of obscene. Don't you remember? You fucked me—"

"Please—"

"All those years ago?"

"You wanted to punish me?"

"Maybe. For not remembering. But, then. If I am to tell the truth, I began to enjoy it."

"So, it's a game with you?"

"No. I enjoyed the house. Your company. And lately, the sound of your playing."

There was something else. Two somethings, actually.

"But do you know what kept me here?"

"You had better tell me."

"The story. That well."

She took her hand away. Made a move towards the front door. His breathing was coming fast, through his nostrils, his mouth clenched shut. She thought of a horse after a race.

"I'll fill it in."

"Don't."

She took one step back. She began to breathe like him.

"Don't go—"

"I won't. I'll finish cleaning up."

"I didn't mean that. I meant."

"I think I know what you meant. But it's a bad idea."

"Why?"

And now it was his turn to wonder. Why had he asked why?

"Because," she said.

★

Because, she was about to say, I had a child.

But she didn't. And afterwards, when things between them got more tangled than the briars around the unweeded garden and the crab apple trees that led to the trellis and the well, she would wonder why she didn't.

Because maybe that's what her well was about. All of the unfinished, untold stories.

He's been trying to reach me, she could have said. I have a letter in my back pocket that's burning a hole into the bum you seemed to like so much.

But she didn't say that either.

So all he could hear was the iambic of her heels across the wooden floor. The creak of the front door when she opened it. The rattle of her bike, down the long avenue of poplar and elm. He looked at the bubbled shape of her red raincoat, in the window.

Something had happened, and he wasn't sure what.

She had left the door open. He stood up from the piano, pulling the robe around him. He raised one hand, to wave goodbye, although she couldn't have seen it. The skin of his fingers seemed to crack, as he clenched them. How long would it last, he wondered, this respite?

As long as he could see her, cycling down that avenue. And her raincoat moved through the gates, the red hood bobbed past the old stone wall until she was gone.

PART TWO

15

He wondered who he was, for the umpteenth time. Waking, with a fly buzzing somewhere above his eyeball, between it and the caravan window. Then he was that fly, with its hundred eyes, high above the scene, looking down on two prone boyish torsos on a mattress, one comatose, one dead. Whichever, there was no problem. There never was a problem with the drug, which again was maybe why they, and everybody, took it. He remembered the old dealer's gaff in Spittal Street, climbing the dingy stairs and seeing one user inject another in the eyeball. How could anyone do that. Now he understood. It was as if everything was felt by someone else, everything had been done to someone else. It was as if someone else had filled the needle, found the vein and injected someone else's arm. And now he drifted, someone else again, above the scene. The needle still hanging from Alastair's arm. So Alastair was the inert one. He was Hughie, the waking one. He could have called a hospital. But he knew he wouldn't. Not yet, anyway. And he wouldn't, not only because he was afraid of the consequences, of a police enquiry. It was because he knew that his Alastair was already in that great place of dislocation that the drug had promised.

He was somewhere else. He always wanted to be somewhere else. He knew little of this euphoric partner, apart from the musings about actual, not adoptive parents, a mother who, as in some *Oliver Twist* fantasy, sat upon some garden of plenty. She was rich, Alastair somehow knew, or had convinced himself, and dwelt, as everyone in Ireland did, in realms of gold.

There was nothing Irish about his accent, though. Hughie at first had thought it was an affectation, the way his own would switch from posh Edinburgh to Begbie's from *Trainspotting* depending on the company he kept. But no, this boy was all Hull, East Yorkshire.

In the Fleece Inn, on the Lock Road in Grimsby. There was a girl between them, what was her name, Rose, Flora, something buttercuppy. Daisy, that was it. She fancied him, not this Alastair, but Alastair was the one who grabbed her when she staggered and led her, hand on elbow, towards the door. He was amazed when the same Alastair came back, having put her in a taxi, and it wasn't consideration either, he wanted what he already knew Hughie had.

He had ended up the way everyone did, dealing the stuff to keep his own habit going and only gradually realizing that this other was learning to do the same. The same pinched face as his, the same angular frame, but without the hard bands of muscle.

So they moved into the caravan together, amongst the small suburb of empty caravans that lined the waterfront in Cleethorpes. Hughie was learning he would have to get used to caravans, if he never got a handle on his habit. Alastair had found them work for a while, painting orange preservative on the oil storage tanks, from platforms that wobbled haphazardly in the wind, sending tins of the paint tumbling down below. And it had been good for a time, the wage envelope on a Friday afternoon, the few pints of cider, the fresh cod and chips before the trawl they knew would eventually happen, through the back streets of Grimsby for whatever was available. The life was temporary, he told himself, there would be other options, but somewhere inside himself he knew all the options would be worse. But he found this new one entrancing, with that odd lisp and that sense of another possible life behind that Yorkshire burr. Alastair. The name was Scottish, which gave them something in common beyond the intermittent desire for oblivion. He always wanted a companion and this one, with a few biographical details added, could well have been his brother. They could imagine each other's lives, when the dope truly took over, how one could well have been the other.

So it had been good for a while, there was money to burn and burn it they did, until one of the paint cans tumbled down and almost knocked the ganger out, dousing his pinstriped suit in the orange rust preservative. It was not quite all downhill from there, there was the respite of a week or two on their wage packets, the bliss of not having to wake each morning, then another month of after-hours dealing, until their level of consumption surpassed their outlays, entirely. Then the quick descent, and then this.

He took the money, of course, without a second thought. Fingering round the pocket of those tight jeans, realizing how little weight was left on the thighs, he found nothing except a few crumpled notes and a coin or two. Sorry, Alastair, he murmured, that you were so reduced. Then he remembered the backpack, found the wallet in the little pouch that included some roll-up tobacco and some folded papers. He hadn't time to separate one from the other so he took the whole pouch. He wondered again about the hospital, and thought if anyone should learn he was gone it should be the parents. There must be a number somewhere in there. And he remembered, again, that they weren't entirely real. That afternoon in the squat in Hull, the sound of playing from the broken piano and the response, when asked where he learned it. I dunno. Always played. Not your parents then? Fuck no. And anyway they weren't my parents. Adopted? Foster parents, he said, do we have to go through that again.

They didn't. He already knew. He wondered what the mindset would be if you had an actual, real and cogent reason to loathe those you were thrown together with at, or just after, birth. He had none. His parents were his parents, no doubt about it. And the loathing was mutual. Almost familiar, like hating a piece of your actual self.

This was on the pebbled beach with the wind coming in from the Hook of Holland or whatever the fuck else was out there beyond those brown choppy waters. There was a fishing boat tossing up and down in them like a lovesick duck and that's when he thought of a solution. What did he know about fishing? As much as he knew about sous-cheffing, and he had blagged his way into a stint in a kitchen or two, supplying them with more than culinary delights. But a stint on one of those, no dealers in sight, cold turkey on the ocean waves. It sounded almost funny, like a Pogues song, but the more he thought of it the more possible it seemed. And that was what he needed then, possibility, any possibility. He had left a dead acquaintance behind on a caravan mattress. As the drugs wore off they left a sense of consequences behind them. So he caught the bus to the waterfront of Hull and when asked for his name by the skipper on the *Lady Eve*, for some reason gave the other's name, Alastair, without any thought whatsoever. Scottish, and at least he had the accent to justify it. The hard Hibs version, not the Edinburgh burr. And when he was told to report later that afternoon, he took out the other's mobile and dialled 999, reported a possible overdose

in the Beachcomber Caravan Park in Cleethorpes. He knew
better than to use his own. Could have been worth something, a
Samsung Galaxy, then he had second thoughts and threw it into
the heaving sea.

And his only relief was being somebody else, shivering in a
southwesterly that was driving them over the Scottish coast. He
wanted to be someone else, he wanted this habit to belong to
some dead thing, he wanted this monkey to be on someone else's
back and to become this new thing, this new self, and Alastair
was as good a name for it as any. He proved useless at trawling so
was relegated to the kitchens, where he could shiver and sweat
to his heart's content, try to keep the DTs at bay with constant
nips of the kitchen brandy. He had always been good at rustling
up a storm, managed a biker's version of a morning fry and a cod
and chorizo stew with whatever other vegetables were available
and kept the coffee brewing. He became, to his surprise, quite
popular amongst the Lithuanians and Poles and Lebanese that
constituted the crew. Alastair, make us up another western. So
Alastair he remained. The odd sense of being somebody else
wasn't so much comforting as a mental trick with which he
managed his withdrawal. It was, like the addiction, happening
to someone else. So when he was deposited in Killybegs Harbour
with four weeks' wages to burn, he effectively was somebody else.
He needed a second name to go with the Alastair and he decided
Brown would do. Alastair Brown, as good a name as any.

He moved south from Killybegs. Migrant birds always moved
south, and he was now a migrant bird. Down the Sligo coast,
through the surfers' caravans that dotted the windswept beaches.
He camped out in another abandoned one of those, and could
have begun plying his old trade here, but the thought of it
repelled him now, like a return to a life he had tossed aside on the

north coast of England. And that's when he opened the wallet in the dead one's pouch. Strange that it had taken him so long, he thought. Maybe he had avoided the idea, like a bad dream, but if that was the case, why had he kept it? He saw the name on the Visa card and had to smile. Hitchens. Alastair Hitchens.

The Visa card proved useful as long as the tab was kept low. It was amazing how simple it was to survive on transactions that hovered below twenty-three euro. Then one afternoon, in Bundoran, even these were refused and he felt a shiver of fear for the first time. He threw the card in a waste bin, and later that night returned, with a paranoia he couldn't shake off. He emptied the waste bin of chip wrappers and old cigarette packets until he found it again. Took it back to the surfer's caravan, thought the pouch might give some clue as to a pin number. A date of birth, maybe, frontways or backways.

There was an old letter, folded around another card, an RBS one this time. From a mother, Christabel, begging him to make up with his father, Francis. He wondered did he call them the same, Christabel and Francis, not Mum and Dad. Then he remembered the dead one's stories of their pride in his recitals on the piano in the stuffy living room, the lessons they had paid for with the insufferable lady, what was her name? Mrs Ffrench. Ffrench with two "f"s. His facility on the keys a constant reminder that wherever he had come from, it wasn't from them. There was a letter from an adoption agency refusing a request for contact and another one from Christabel, the mum, who had traced a woman called Tara, a piano teacher in a town called Orran.

There was a date of birth, indeed, the first four numbers of which unlocked the riches of the Visa. So he thought he would travel south, to acquaint himself with a life the other could have lived.

He remembered the sound of the barely tuned piano from the squat in Hull. Midges drifting in the afternoon wedge of sunlight. What are you playin', piano man? Chopin, came the reply. So he revived his Spotify account and began to listen to a different world of music on his journey south. Less acid house and trap, more pianists with Russian unpronounceable names. It lulled him on the bus journey to Galway, blocked out the sounds of buskers on Eyre Square, and by the time he reached Limerick he could almost feel the soul of his dead acquaintance had entered him. Friend was the wrong word, he knew; they had been tied by something other than friendship, a mutual need for a narcotic experience that was stronger than both of them. And anytime he felt the pull, as he did outside the McDonald's, O'Connell Street, Limerick, he would allow the same piano sounds to massage his ears. It would have been so easy, the youths in hoodies smoking cigarettes by the rubbish bins, he could feel the presence of it the way a fox could smell out chickens, but he allowed the piano to work its magic and the image of the dead one's mother to console him. Tara, the name itself sounded more Irish than Ireland, the name of the house in some old movie, what was it called again, *Gone with the Wind*. He could imagine a face, beautiful, of course, the way a real mother's was. Not his own mother, no, not that drawn cigarette-smoking visage, this one was softer, reddish-haired, with greenish eyes, and at that thought he felt stupid, he was in Ireland, did he have to make her reddish-haired, auburn, that was the better word, and why, for god's sake, the green eyes? But they persisted, they stuck, once imagined. The name of the town on the address he had seen scribbled. Orran. It sounded Gallic or Nordic, but there it was, he was at the outer end of things, and besides, he wasn't himself any longer. He wasn't Alastair Brown either. He didn't know who he was. He took another bus then to a town called Bantry and another one before his money ran out and he finally reached it. Orran.

Why was he here again? He kept forgetting the reason. Maybe he needed to score after all, to get that certainty back. There was a small harbour, with boats covered in those canvas coverings for the winter. He felt guilt, perhaps. Someone had died, whose mother might live here. He thought he'd try the credit card again, and walked into the supermarket and was surprised to find it so well appointed. There were craft beers, bottles of wine that cost more than the best single malt scotch, and indeed, bottles of single malt scotch that cost more than all of them. He bought a can of cider and thought he would try paying for it with Alastair's RBS. It went through, to his relief, and he could have kicked himself then, he should have at least added a bag of crisps. He pointed then to a box of Amber Leaf, and the girl in the blue and yellow outfit ran it through again, and to his relief, it went through again. Things were looking up, he felt, and ambled outside and sat on the café bench on the street with the view of the harbour, cracked open the can and rolled himself one.

He wondered what to do with the idea of Alastair. He was Hughie no longer, Hitchens was what the Visa card read. Could he even attempt to be Alastair Hitchens? He owed a debt of kinds to the dead one. A debt to a death. It was funny, how two words that sounded almost the same could be so different. There was a mother here, who didn't know her son was dead. Who didn't know her son, for reasons he could obscurely imagine. Ireland, shame, mother and baby homes, forced adoptions, he had seen the movie, read the reports in the *Daily Mirror* and the *Sun*. But yet. He had been brought up in England, in a suburb of Hull to be precise, by Christabel and Francis Hitchens. There had been piano lessons and even, if he could bear to recall those narcotic afternoons, something about a boarding school. His Alastair's story wasn't one of sadistic nuns and rapacious Christian Brothers. It was one of caring, adoptive parents, a middle-class street – and he could picture it if he closed his eyes. Those high-gabled semi-detached houses with cherry trees in the gardens. Yes, cherries, he thought. There would have to be cherry blossoms. Ending in a rupture. There had to have been a rupture, else why would he and the father have to make up?

He could imagine the blossoms falling, in the spring, when Christabel took young Alastair out walking. One of those harnesses with reins that young mothers used then. The boy trying to run, the mother uncertain she should let him, the cherry blossoms falling all around them. Pink on the green garden lawns. When did cherry blossoms fall?

It was interesting, being someone else. It relieved him of the burden of being himself, which he now realized was always a terrible one. Although this other was not quite Alastair and not quite him. It was something in between. He wondered was that how actors felt, when they were searching for a character. And that word, character, reminded him of his own, his real father. He had always lacked character, that father said.

Well, maybe he could find it now.

Then he heard the sound of a squeaking bicycle. Someone had come to a halt and was adjusting a chain, or a lock.

The minute he saw her, he knew. How did he know? Need had seeped through Alastair like rust from copper, like pus through a bandage.

She was a mother. She had mother hidden inside her, like blood from a bandaged wound.

Maybe it was the sandy hair, barely hiding the thin, elongated neck.

But it wasn't entirely physical, she didn't look a lot like him, she was a woman, for god's sake, a woman of the right age. And there was something in her way of walking, after she had perched her bike by the bench outside the coffee shop. A kind of a rolling walk, as if the earth beneath her feet was somehow uncertain. Her Alastair had the same, that sailor's roll, and if she had been made of chewing gum and a capricious child had stretched her, he could imagine her becoming him.

He heard the voice from the café inside. What's the story, Tara?

And what was the story, he began to wonder? How does a woman abandon the body he himself abandoned back in faraway England? But she didn't abandon the adult, she abandoned the child. The newborn.

There was a death to be paid, he thought to himself. Or a debt.

16

She didn't come for three weeks. He allowed the dishes to pile in the sink, while he tried to enjoy the unfamiliar silence, practised scales relentlessly, as if afraid that any relaxation of his schedule would bring the affliction back. But it didn't. His skin remained supple and uncracked, his fingers stretched with a fluidity that would have amazed a younger player. He wandered out every third night and pulled fistfuls of moss from the dripping walls of the well. Sometimes there was a moon. He imagined the hare observing him, and once or twice whirled round as if to catch it in its act of moonlit dancing, but there was never anything there.

Perhaps it followed her, he began to think, and with the same thought came another, that he missed her. He walked back inside and began to clean the sink, using that eco-detergent that she had bought. For times like this, he wondered, when she wouldn't be around?

His anger had subsided. Though whether he or she had more right to such an emotion was a moot point. He could remember the piano competition dimly, the flight to Dublin, the taxi drive underneath that oppressive bridge, the hotel near the government buildings, and even the name, Buswells. He could remember the dusty hall, the table behind which he sat with the music professor from Trinity and the portly local version of Rubenstein, but nothing else. Nothing of the participants and definitely nothing of their hands. The Wigmore Hall in London became his local refuge from the grind of touring, he must have played there twice, three times a year over three decades, how many flutes of champagne had he shared with ardent fans, and how many had he slept with, all of them forgotten.

But she had told him it hadn't happened there.

He remembered his battle with the Shostakovich preludes in the Brighton Dome only because he lost it. Too austere for that middlebrow audience, a bad choice anyway, Tchaikovsky might have brought them huzzawing to their feet. He could only remember that nobody noticed his failure, the applause was polite and respectable. Of the woman he had met later in the Grand Hotel bar, he could piece together nothing. Oh, he could force some memory out of a few random encounters. How many had there been, in how many hotel rooms, some of them no doubt in Brighton, and he was a touring musician after all. She had noticed he played badly, she said. The only discerning one amongst that audience, so he should have remembered. But did she tell him that then? No, she told him that later. Three weeks ago, to be exact.

So he remembered nothing of her then, but he remembered everything of her now. And it was odd, the emptiness it caused. He was used to emptiness of course, isolation, a transient life, he had long steeled himself against a certain kind of need. Loneliness is how you perceive it, he had long told himself, trained himself to enjoy his own company, his own habits. Perhaps too successfully, which must be why his marriage had failed.

He cleaned the kitchen one evening and when the feeling became unbearable, he recognized it for what it was. His old companion, isolation. But what had been a familiar kind of retreat was now a cold condition. He could imagine long, sustained drips coming from some ungodly aperture above. As if he was sitting at the bottom of something, some place he had been all his life headed towards. And he thought of the well. Wondered could he be, as in some sleight of hand they employed in movies, sitting in the pit of that.

He walked outside. There was an intermittent moon, dancing between the windblown clouds. Each gust brought tumbles of dark descending leaves. And there was the well, inside its haphazard fencing. Something across the grasses, looking towards the well, or him. Something that appeared and disappeared with the moonlight. And from the upright ears he recognized what it was, from a remembered illustration in some fairy tale.

So it hadn't gone with her, the hare.

And that's when he knew he had to see her again.

17

She felt she was being watched, and of course wondered was it William. Inside the café, pulling on her mask, a silhouetted figure, hunched on the bench outside. But it couldn't be, he would never be that adolescent, and anyway, when she exited with her cappuccino, whoever it was had gone.

Crossing the street towards the butcher's shop, she heard the sound of a car, and kept walking in case it was his Jaguar. She saw then, out of the corner of her eye, a battered HiAce van round the bend and out of sight and realized it wasn't. She felt a strange disappointment, then a more familiar pang of guilt. She should have called to say she wasn't coming, even as a professional courtesy, but for all of the obvious reasons, couldn't. Why she felt the guilt that should have more properly been his was a mystery to her. She had responded to his notice, taken the job, done it to the best of her abilities, kept herself to herself. Until that business with the hole in the ground. She could have finished after a month or so, seen what his life was like, gained whatever satisfaction she desired through the state of him, his hands useless, his piano untouched, his career finished. But that wasn't the whole story, of course not. There was a residue of something else that it took the well to suck out of her.

She remembered that afternoon in the clinic when she stood

up on some impulse and turned to leave. The matter-of-fact receptionist asking was she OK, and she replied fine, I'll be back tomorrow, or something like it. The train then, back to Brighton and two days of blessed freedom to consider what she'd done. She knew why of course, it was the residue from that enormous hall of a church on the Drumcondra Road, some mention of her mother's of whitethorn along the tracks of the West Clare railway. She didn't want to be bound by some duty to an unlived life but couldn't resist it. She knew, with a dull certainty, that she had no other choice. Her bass player came back then, with his bitten nails and his tobacco-stained fingers from some tour around Sheffield. Surprised, of course. Indifferent, whether it was his or not. It was her decision. And as her body grew, his declined. His habit grew, his body didn't so much shrivel as occupy less space. He left one day, it was a Thursday she remembered, his and her dole day, which could have been the reason. Two payments gone from the glass table by the television and a note, almost poignant in its brevity. You do your thing I'll do mine. Love, Jack.

She told her mother, an endless succession of coins into the payphone in the corridor. Her mother had the grace not to be surprised. Don't tell your father. You're in England, isn't that where they deal with those things? She didn't call again. She contacted an adoption agency, which helped with the hospital arrangements, and once again was amazed at the practical, straightforward care they devoted to her situation. She had the child on a Tuesday morning of a springtime. She knew it was springtime by the spring cherries outside of her bedroom window.

She left the hospital soon after and was surprised at how free she felt. Maybe there was something wrong with her. The sense of lightness as she walked along the promenade only increased as her body returned to normal. Was it the absence of those leather trousers in the basement of her Brighton flat? He was gone, the child was gone and she would have to think about the latter sometime, but not now. The former hardly bore thinking about, but the absence of those little burnt paper foils and the occasional needle and the ruptured sleep and the night sweats, the talk about rehab, all seemed like a new life to her. The payphone rang in the corridor one day and it was him, needing to pick up an oscillator or a transformer or a flange pedal – she never understood those terms – and she told him come any time. So she opened the door when the bell rang and walked outside and smoked in the back garden, while he rummaged around. He must have found it, because she heard the door slam and squashed her cigarette in the grass and made her way back inside.

She could smell him, like an old bad habit. Was the child his? He imagined so, and hence his disquiet. Not at the loss of it, and he would only refer to it as "it", but at the possibility of it. Was she insane? The world had enough on its shoulders without this. But she had given birth and given it up, all in the same few days, and they were both out of her life now. She had been dreading the endless discussions of their trauma and the fear that in the course of them she might reveal her real suspicion, that the child wasn't his.

She grew plants in his studio, wallpapered with eggshell boxes. She took pupils in there too, on the piano which sat happily amongst the ever growing foliage, and when the rent was upped to a level that she knew was unsustainable because the landlord wanted to sell the house above, she left Brighton for good. The place was changing anyway, a new affluence was in the air, the rows of boarding houses being sold to accommodate young families from London. The young mothers with their three-wheeled buggies, babies no older than her own, would have been straining to burst out of them.

She returned to Dublin for her father's funeral. She stood by the flattened grave on a wet afternoon in Howth and wondered why her mother hadn't chosen an upright one, like that forest of dark marble in Glasnevin Cemetery.

And her wandering began, as if she were trying to escape something. Back to London, from the drab brown vista of the Drumcondra Road, then the oddest of jobs, playing piano on a cruise ship, which took her through the Norway fjords to Miami and Antigua and left her like an out-of-water fish in San Francisco. There was a small Irish community there, carpenters and expat journalists and a defrocked priest she met working a bar in the Tenderloin. He managed the place and eventually bought it, and always threatened a relationship which she kept at bay with her suspicion that he was, or would one day turn out to be, gay. She left again before she could find out, back to Dublin for her mother's funeral and her discovery that amongst her inheritance was this small cottage above the harbour in a West Cork village. She travelled down there, found it pleasant though in need of renovation, in the course of which she found herself moving in.

If anyone had asked her why she stayed, she couldn't have given a straight or succinct answer. But it wasn't in their habit there to ask such questions. They assumed the felicities of the one-street town were their own justification. So she stayed, and stopped asking herself.

Erik squawked as she entered the front door and called out her name, "Tara". She whistled the bar of Satie back at him and said hello to her old life. She was taking lessons again, and tried to remember who was due at twelve.

18

The house. It looked like a mother's house, although he realized any house could look like a mother's house. He watched the bicycle flit between the shapes of summer bungalows, round a semi-circle of two storeys that led to a small lane between dry stone walls. A cottage then, backing onto a straggling thicket of trees.

He made his way round the side and heard someone call a greeting as she opened the front door. Not a child, for sure. Maybe a husband. Or what was the word they all used these days? Partner.

And although there were no plastic toys in the garden and not even one of those triangular clothes drying things in the backyard, it all had the feeling of mother somehow. Or maybe the smell. Or maybe it was, around midday, after he had walked past it four times, down to the small windswept harbour with the pebbled beach behind it and back again, when he saw the boy with the music case amble up, push aside the squeaking gate with his knee and bang the music case three times off the door, that he thought, she has another child, of course, why not, the one thing I didn't think of. He saw her answer the door then in a way that was not like a mother at all, but it was odd these days, mothers could look as desirable as any young lithe thing, and when she admitted the boy, he made his way round the back. He heard the sound of the piano then, and a cock crowed somewhere in the gardens beyond and he felt, not for the first time, that he was in another country, where all of the signs were different.

He would have to get used to reading them if he was ever to knock on the door and introduce himself. Then there was the question of what he would say. Hello, I left your son dead on a mattress in Cleethorpes, next to Grimsby, which was down from Hull on the Humber. No, not that. Definitely not that. Why did he always think of it as Hull on the Humber, it was just fucking Hull, the river didn't matter, not to the transient he had been anyway, it was the place where the smack was sometimes laced with fentanyl, cheaper than it was in Leith. And maybe that was what had done it for her boy, the fentanyl, not the brown. He had a part to play, if they ever got to speak, and the words were not hello I left your son dead on a mattress in Cleethorpes, the words were hello I am your son from Hull on the Humber and Alastair is my name.

Maybe that was why he walked back up to that dismal main street and ordered a coffee from the coffee shop. He had to think about these things. And maybe think was the wrong word, he had to let them circle in his head the way underwear would circle in a dryer in a laundromat. And he had paid for it and was blowing the chocolate from the froth when he saw the red-peaked hoodie wheel the bicycle up the hill and he saw her mount it on the main street. It wasn't a hoodie, more of a plastic raincoat because it didn't ruffle in the breeze that whipped away the chocolate on the froth of his coffee cup. That was another thing, he hadn't asked for chocolate, it had just appeared, another strange habit in this country he would have to learn about. Maybe they all expected it. No chocolate, no sugar.

So she was home no longer. She had to work, of course, we all have to work, and she cycled to wherever work was. She wouldn't have made the Tour de France, he could see that, she cycled the way a mother would despite the slim figure and the unlikely red hoodie thing, slowly, as if each pedal down was an effort. And when she vanished round the small streets on the rise of the main street he finished his coffee in one gulp and made his way back to her house. It was drawing him in now, like a new drug on the market that he had never tried, and he wondered why. Was it to do with the dead one whose name he had taken, whose person he was wearing like a borrowed cloak? Had he a message to give her? About the one she abandoned? And then he realized, with a dull ache, that they had that in common. So he walked over the childless lawn with no evidence of toys, put one hand against his eyes to peer in the front window, saw a piano there and almost ran when he heard the loud whistle, followed by a squawk, and realized it was a parrot in a cage, perched on the dark wood.

He would have let it go then, but the parrot whistled, some kind of tune, and it sounded familiar so he walked round the back.

The back garden was in better shape. Small rows of vegetables, a potato patch and a potted plant by the door which all too obviously hid a key beneath it.

Now I would never dream of looking there, he mused, as he turned the key in the back door lock.

A small, neat kitchen with a lightly humming fridge.

Another whistle, of that same tune from the parrot inside and it was like an earworm now, he couldn't trace where he had heard it. Some chocolate box commercial. But it suited the small hallway, the threadbare carpet of the stairs heading up to his left towards her bedroom, he imagined, and he tried to picture to himself what her bedroom would look like.

Into the living room then, the small upright piano, of course, there would have to be a piano, with a squiggle board above it and a list of names and times.

A piano teacher, of course. The small boy was a pupil, not a son from a second family. There was a warmth to the place, a sense of completeness, he was good at reading people and places, breaking and entering wasn't his thing, but he could read the signs. And this was an oddly serene house, for a mother who had abandoned her Alastair all of those years ago. He walked into the hallway and back to the kitchen, pulled open the drawer beneath the kitchen table and began to scour the letters there. He lifted one, half opened. He took Alastair's own letter out, crumpled from his pocket, and was looking for a postmark or a matching address, just to be sure for whatever the future might hold, he didn't want to stalk the wrong one did he, when he heard the front door open, had to stop himself from running.

Four quiet steps, to the kitchen door, and a vault across the garden wall and it wasn't until he was back on the field outside that he realized he had the wrong letter in his hand.

19

Again, the sense that she was being watched. And she was, as the intruder made his way across the adjacent garden onto the small lane that led to her front door. There was a mottled shape inside the glass that made its way into the kitchen and lost all shape altogether.

She missed the regular contact, she supposed, so much so that she had cycled towards the rectory, and only corrected her foolishness when the line of trees made their appearance over the old stone wall.

William was in there, she supposed, practising with his new hands which she herself could take some credit for. Some badly needed form of autosuggestion, unless she was to believe her own inventions about the well, its water, its magically healing mosses. So there. It was that easy to plant a seed in a parched landscape and his must have been parched indeed. But she missed something, whether it was the play of some kind of long delayed romantic retribution, the presence of his languid English self, his finished sentences. That it had taken so long to reveal itself surprised her. What was the point of the whole arrangement, if not some form of revenge? But something had happened, something that surprised even her own dead emotional self. So the final twisting of the blade never arrived.

I had a child. And it is possible, probable even, that you are the father. More than probable, if she really examined herself. In some deep well inside her – and there was that word again, it had lately seemed to apply everywhere – she knew.

She hadn't told him. She wouldn't tell him. What would be the point, in the inevitable self-laceration it would give rise to. Besides which, it would entangle her further with him, and with all of that, she was finished.

So where came this sense to her that she was being watched? He would never follow her here surely, unless it was possible that inside the same William Barrow there was a needy adolescent, capable of the irrational emptiness she had experienced all of those years ago. But there were eyes on her, she could feel it. The parrot gave an unfamiliar squawk before his familiar attempt at the first three bars of the Satie. She opened the kitchen door and saw the letter on the floor.

From the Adoption Contact Register. To Alastair Hitchens, Sutton Gardens, Kingston Upon Hull.

"This is not a tracing service," she read. "For a connection to be made between people, you must both be on the Adoption Contact Register."

Instructions, then, as to how to register.

She wondered, the way someone would wonder about someone else, had Alastair Hitchens registered himself. She wondered should she. All before it hit her, with the force of a sudden rush of blood, that he had been here.

She had to sit. But she saw the drawer beneath the kitchen table half open, and realized he had not only been here but had been rummaging through her things. The familiar chair seemed to carry an odour, even a threat. She walked back out, letter in hand, and took her seat beside the piano.

She ran her hands over the keys. Had he been sitting here too? Did he even play these keys?

Did you hear him play, Erik, she asked and she didn't even smile at the absurdity of questioning a parrot.

She needed to think. And more than that, she needed to breathe.

She walked back through the hallway, through the kitchen, in which she was now certain she could catch the odour of an unfamiliar being, and opened the back door. She saw the damp half-circle where the potted plant had been shifted. She bent down and lifted the key.

Well, at least, she thought, he left her that.

She walked down through the vegetable patches. She took in deep breaths. She could see the flecked white horses on the Atlantic Ocean. Several fishing boats bobbing there, one of which was probably Peter's.

20

He had dropped the letter by accident, he was sure of that. But it was one of those accidents that had a hidden purpose. What was the purpose? He wasn't sure of that. Had the ghost of the real Alastair let it fall? Anyway, there was a debt to be paid. Had he placed the letter carefully on the wooden table, scribbled her name with a little note, "Your darling son", he could not have repaid that debt more completely. Less, what was the word, surreptitiously. And he had two options now, to get the fuck out of there before something started, or to stay and observe how it continued. He looked at the mistaken envelope, the name it was addressed to: Tara Stafford. He pulled out the letter inside and saw the same name, with a credit card cunningly inserted into four incisions in the paper. Pin number by separate post.

He could trundle back to that port on the other peninsula, he could get a berth on a boat that would take him to Holland or Spain or the Bay of Biscay, wherever that was, or back to Hull on the fucking Humber. But he was not really the fish-hauling type, and another two weeks in a trawler's kitchen didn't really appeal to him. So he decided to stay. He had two credit cards to play with, though he doubted the mother's would be based on any birth date, even if he could discover it. He walked into the local SuperValu and used the dead one's plastic to get more supplies and headed outside, both hands full of supermarket bags, as the night was coming down. He made his way to the small excuse for a harbour and trod a path along the stony, cobbled shore. He found an empty summer caravan amongst a copse of ash trees, but it wasn't summer was it, it wouldn't be summer for a while, so he kicked the door open and made himself at home. He pulled the sleeping bag from his backpack and laid it out on the stretch of deal that seemed designed for a bed. He could see the yellow gleam of a Kosangas canister beneath a gas ring. It would be empty, of course, but he could get it filled at the station in the morning. He cracked a Heineken can and wondered what of his purchases he would have for dinner.

He wasn't the trawling type, he had to realize that. He was more the observing type, and he was genuinely curious as to how this little story of theirs would play out. It wasn't his story, of course, it was his dead companion's, but it was becoming his story bit by bit. And he owed a duty to the deceased one, he felt, to follow it through. To report back, in a sense. Can one tell a story to the dead? What was his name again? Alastair, of course, Alastair Hitchens.

He thought of his own father, who ran a bitumen and emulsion plant in Leith, and said he had always lacked that thing he was searching for now, that thing called character. The smell of the molten tar did sicken him when the huge concrete tubes came dripping from the vats, and he supposed one who didn't lack character would have been able to endure those fumes. Did he lack it now, he wondered, being Alastair? He knew as little of him as he did of himself, but he had the odd feeling, as he drifted off to sleep, that with Alastair would come that strange elusive character that he had always lacked.

He awoke to find a jackdaw pecking at the plastic window,

one of those that only opened a sliver no matter how you pushed it. He could break it with a handy brick, if the heat got too much in summer. But would he still be here, come summer? He had the feeling that Alastair definitely would.

He rummaged round the caravan wondering what bits and pieces whoever the owners were had left. He lifted the wooden cover beneath his sleeping bag and saw a tangle of fishing line and hooks in the underbed storage thing beneath. What was it called? There must be a word for that cluttered space, he thought, and began to untangle the dulled plastic lines of gut. It was complicated by the fact that there were hooks, every arm-length or so of knotted line. He then saw the yards of fishing line were hiding two knotted staves of metal with eye-sockets at the top and realized he had found a ready-made set of nightlines. He remembered laying similar lines on the beach at Newhaven with his father, who, he realized, never lacked that thing called character. Their uneasy sleep under the canvas tent was always leavened by the discovery next morning of a dozen or so flapping plaice, sole or flounder with the odd crab or two still clinging for dear life. He could try the ocean here, and see if it would be forthcoming with what his father always called its bounty.

He gathered the whole unruly assemblage in his arms, laid it out on the grass outside the caravan steps, and wound them carefully, one rod in a ball of fishing line and hooks towards the other.

He could see a thin sliver of silver through the ash trees which he knew was the retreating tide. So he walked down with his arms full of rods, hooks and catgut, towards the shore.

The scalloped surface of the dark sand, with the runnels of water flowing backwards, as the tide went out. He heard the squelch of each trainer on the wet surface, and knew his feet would get wet, but kept going. There would be a present at the end of it all, if not today, then definitely tomorrow. And who knew, the Atlantic might give him what the North Sea never did. That elusive catch called character.

There were a few distant, silhouetted figures digging on the shoreline. A dog, running and barking between them. Foragers, he imagined, maybe even strangers to the place like him. He dug, like them, wherever the wormcasts showed. He drove one metal rod into the wet sculpted sand and hammered it down with his bent elbow, his parka bunched like a protective pillow beneath it. Then he unwound the gut-threaded hooks, and did the same with the other rod. He wormed each hook, then began the walk back, and turned to survey his enterprise. Two staffs that could have been wielded by Moses, and a thin line of baited hooks, shifting darkly between them.

21

She sat in her kitchen table and smoked, with the letter before her. She had to admire the tone of it, the official rebuff, not entirely free of sympathy. She had often thought of making a similar enquiry, and was glad to learn that they were not a tracing service, that her first step would have to be to place her name and address with the Adoption Contact Register. Then she saw the barely perceptible smudge of a shoe, a trainer probably, on the floor below the letter in her hand and felt the blood retreat from wherever it should have been and realized again that she had been invaded. An intruder, the dried flecks of mud that barely outlined a shoeprint on her tiled kitchen floor. She should call the police, she realized then, they could match that print with her own son's footwear, Adidas, Asics, whatever his taste happened to be. And the implication of that thought hit her even more, not the word son, but the implied reality of it, which for two decades she had forgotten. She had a mother hidden somewhere inside herself. Where Peter, Mary, even William, god help him, saw a not unattractive woman moving capriciously into middle age, there was an unseen element, a dark water that would someday be whipped into a wave and erupt, the way the waters of that well seemed to do from the blowhole. She had a son, and he had been here. She could call the police, but she knew instinctively that nothing had been taken, he had come in the spirit of some kind of enquiry, had left that letter as the first, hesitant attempt at a conversation that would have to be had, someday. And besides, how can you call the law on your own flesh and blood?

She felt the urge to cycle up again to the rectory, the need to talk to somebody, but realized that if she did just that, she wouldn't, she couldn't share this dilemma with William Barrow. She would end up talking to that dark cylinder of moss that she had so playfully named Saint Ite's Well.

She glanced once more at the letter. Addressed to Alastair Hitchens.

Alastair. He had a name, at least, given to him by the Hitchens, whoever they were. Adoptive parents. She could only hope they served him well.

She rose from the table, took a J-cloth from the sink, dampened it with tap water and fell to her knees and scrubbed her Alastair's print from the kitchen tiles. Whatever came between them, she dimly thought, would not be legal.

She walked into the front room and sat by the keys, her fingers rippling over them in indeterminate scales. She heard Erik the parrot whistle his five good notes and asked him idly, without turning round, had he seen this Alastair, intruder on their private space. He whistled again, which told her that he had and she turned and looked at her own reflection in his Mesolithic pupil.

She hardly slept that night. She tossed and turned, out of fractured dreams that had no real definition. She decided to abandon the effort at sleep for good when the first light came through her curtained window. She got up, slipped out of her sweat-clinging things and had a cold shower. She had to clear her head and talk to someone.

William was not appropriate, Mary was impossible, since she would tell the whole of Main Street. Peter was the only option. So she dressed, walked through the whey-coloured dawn down to the cottage that she knew he rented. There was no reply to her knock, it was empty, then she remembered he sometimes slept in the boat, so walked down to the small harbour.

There were a few covered pleasure crafts there, waiting for summer, but no trawler. He could be out lobster potting, she thought, and walked through the straggly forest of trees, down the shaly slope towards the shore. There were boats on the far horizon, but nothing round the bobbing buoys of the lobster pots. He was out on the pelagic somewhere, she realized, remembering that word from their early days. Then she saw two black staves, silhouetted by the rising pale milky sun, with the flapping outlines of fish dangling between them.

Something about the fish reminded her of her parrot's Mesolithic eye. Something ancient, something hidden by the ocean's surface, then offered up, as the sea retreated. She walked towards them. Flatfish, she saw, with one crab that finally gave up its clawed hold and whatever bait had attracted it, fell to the wet sand and scurried back to its remembered ocean home. There was one spiked, double-eyed thing that still had significant life in it, trembled and shivered, leaving tendrils of drops to spatter the wet sand.

She came closer, touched it with her hand. It gave one last twist, as if to stab her palm with its Neanderthal bones, and she pulled her hand back.

She heard a voice behind her.

John Dory, it said.

She turned and saw the trainers squelching over the wet scallops of the sand. As she raised her eyes, she saw a bucket, then a rubber glove, then the torso of a youth that could have been any youth, the rather pimpled, angular face that could have been anyone's. William's, maybe, she thought. He had very little of her.

"You're Alastair," she said.

"Yes," he said, and for the umpteenth time marvelled at how easy it was to lie. Much easier than the truth.

"You were in my kitchen."

"I was. I'm sorry. But you weren't there."

"That's breaking and entering. A crime," she said.

"Well," he said, "very few of us are innocent."

He came close to her. And she, oddly enough, felt nothing, as he placed the bucket down on the sand beside her, and began to jerk the fish from the hooks that had tricked them.

"Where did you learn this?" she asked him.

"Nightlines," he said. "From my father."

"Was he a good father?"

"He thought so," he said. "But then, like in most things, I had no choice."

It was interesting how easy it all was. Though easy wasn't really the word. Suggestive. Each little move on his part led to a corresponding one on hers. As if she had been waiting, like an audience, for this moment. And all he had to do was turn up.

"I'm sorry," she said.

"For what?" he asked.

"For everything," she said.

"Well, I'm sorry too," he said. "For breaking and entering. You have to understand—"

"You were curious?" she said.

"I was. And am. Aren't you?"

There was no answer to that. And as if he understood her lack of curiosity, he pulled one last fish from its bloodied hook. The spiked one.

"Here," he said. "John Dory. For you."

"What am I to do with it?" she asked, stupidly.

"Cook it. Bit of olive oil and some garlic. You and your man-friend."

"Man-friend?"

"Don't you have one?"

There was no reply to that either.

"Mind the bones."

And he placed the fish in her open, surprised hands.

22

She had always loathed fish, but felt she should cook this one. So she skinned it, filleted it and dumped the resultant carcass in the bin beside the sink. She imagined the two adjacent eyes staring at her from the tangled rubbish. If his eyes could see through its dead eyes he would have had a pornographic view of her knees, her skirt and everything above it. What an insane thought, she realized, a dead fish's carcass as avatar to a returned child. But her thoughts weren't making sense to her lately and she might have to resign herself to all sorts of warps in the membrane of ordinary things. However she had imagined the event, and she realized she had kept all imaginings about it effectively at bay, none of the feelings she had were appropriate to it. She felt invaded, ruptured, and savaged by guilt, all at the same time. The olive oil spat on the bubbling pan, she chopped garlic and dropped in the pieces, which browned almost immediately; she laid in the fish fillets, squeezed in some lemon which sputtered in turn and the whole procedure seemed to be spitting things at her, tiny globules of oil and exploding bulbs of lemon, and then the odour, not so much of burning flesh as of roasting seaweed. She turned them with the wooden ladle, scooped them onto a plate and sat down to eat at the table in the kitchen, which no longer felt like her own.

Would she have to share it with this stranger, and maybe that's why he came, were there certain rights of inheritance she had never bothered to make herself aware of? A cottage in an Irish village in this day and age would have some allure, might alone be the reason he sought her out. But no, of course there was something else, the thing she didn't feel at all, the blood connection, motherhood, the something bond, what was the word, filial. Or did filial apply only to men? She would have to speak to someone, Peter maybe, and then she thought of William again, but she didn't want to think of William until she sorted out her feelings which were like a storm brewing inside her, so much of a storm that her hands were shaking and she almost dropped the plate with its filleted John Dory on the floor. At which point she forced herself to calm down, to take up the fork and try a bite.

And the taste was so delicious, it confused her even more. The soft flaky feeling of what could have been the deep ocean, it crumbled in her mouth with the crunchy feel of the roasted garlic and the aftertaste of lemon. She was a meat person, never a fish person; the inert diamonds of white flesh with the white sauce they always seemed to come with didn't bear thinking of, let alone preparing and cooking. And now there was this. What if she had denied herself a whole sliver of the life around her, for unexamined reasons? What if this bountiful thing was hers for the taking, with the added excitement of discovery? What if, in the middle of her life, she had found a new sensation, a new taste and, to use the cliché, she had never known what she was missing? And what if he wasn't an intruder, an invader, but a messenger, a familiar that she should have sought out years ago?

And she really had to speak to someone. Now.

23

She cycled out to the rectory, as the late evening light stretched itself above her. She could have called, but somehow didn't trust her mobile. Besides, she realized, as the elm and poplar trees came into view, they hadn't yet spoken on the telephone. Their conversations had been overheard by nobody, registered on no device whatsoever. The thought gave her an odd kind of comfort. There was something that was hers alone, that would live and die with her.

There was no car in the forecourt, which gave her an odd sort of pang. Maybe he had gone, forever. Back to that place where they finished their sentences, where the passions were more rational. And in a way, she thought, as she dismounted her bike and pushed it up the avenue, she would blame him for so doing.

For so doing, she thought again. Such an English phrase, it could have come from his mouth.

Behind her, he ducked his way over a stone wall and into a field, keeping pace with her, loping through the yellow flowered weeds and avoiding the cowpats. The stone wall between him and her and then a line of ash trees or poplars, then a gate and a paddock and an enclosure of moaning cows. He could have scurried through them but didn't want to be noticed, didn't want to muddy his trainers, so he lost sight of her, made it back over the dry stone wall to the road and jogged along the soft shoulder until he saw two large ornate gateposts, gates hanging between them, already open, and two lines of trees, in the centre of which her bicycle pushed its unsteady way.

He watched her get off, push the bike up the avenue instead of cycling, for some reason. She must have been tired, he thought, or was enjoying the walk amongst the long shadows of the avenue trees. Her own shadow danced between them, the small hood of the red coat making the shadow of a second head. She laid the bike to rest on the pillar of the overhanging thing, what was it called, the portico, and he saw her knock and saw her knock and wait, then scribble a note against one of the pillars, and slip it through what must have been the post box flap.

He couldn't see from the low stone wall, but he could imagine. Then he saw her grip the handle of the bike as if to cycle back, when something changed her mind. She wheeled it as she walked, past the two great windows at the front, laid it against the side and made her way through a tangled garden. She lay down amongst the weeds then and vanished from view.

She could see the long cylindrical fall of the glistening moss in the departing light. It would be quite dark soon and she wanted to have finished what she had to say before the light went entirely. For William to find her here would be more than an embarrassment, it would demand answers and she wanted to tell the unseen waters beneath her what she had to say.

The blood was flowing to her head, dangling as it was over the edge of the stone rim around the well, and she told it everything.

She told it all the hopes of her small hands as she prepared for that competition in the Father Matthew Hall. She told it all the boredom of her days in that Brighton basement flat, as she listened to the electric hum of the bass guitar in the room next door. She told it of her hesitation in the Marie Stopes clinic and the strange decision she made to turn and walk away. The child was the tattooed bassist's or the elegant pianist's, it was somebody's, it would be born and afterwards wouldn't be hers. She told it of the difficulty of playing the *Tritsch-Tratsch Polka* on a shifting ocean liner while the unshapely dancers slipped around an unsteady floor. She told it of her leaden surprise, after her mother's funeral, when she first entered the cottage in Orran. Of the strange feeling of recognition, shock and then of inevitability when she saw those mismatched socks outside the coffee shop on that March day, which seemed years ago now. She told it things she wouldn't have told anyone living, then let her head loll down into the emptiness, exhausted by the telling.

And all the while she was observed, by the youth in the soft trainers moving quietly around the ragwort, under the crab apple trees, and, when she eventually raised her head, behind the rotting wood of some kind of gardening shed. He saw her stand, pull the red hood over her pert head, and make her way back to the side of the large rambling house, where her bicycle waited. He saw her mount it, cycle back that long avenue through the barely perceptible trees, and wondered did she have a light. He saw the yellow glow of a lamp that came on as the bicycle turned, left, back the way she had come, and he realized she had one.

It was almost too easy to enter that mansion. It was the only word he had for a place like this, with the window, buckled by years of damp, the paint flaking off around the wooden frame that he managed to ease free and push up towards the lintel, before it jammed. But it left enough space for him to squirm inside, into that mansion-like smell, old varnished wood and carpet and a dark thing across the way to the left by the other window, what was it, a piano, of course. A grand one this time, with the black top opened up like an enormous shield, held in place by a rod of some kind that seemed designed for the purpose. So they both played, she some kind of teacher with a small, uptight one, he some kind of master with this Rolls-Royce of instruments. He remembered again the sound of the barely tuned piano in the squat in Hull. What are you playin', piano man? And he wondered what the story really was. He wandered round the dark house, into the kitchens, up into the bedrooms above; he would steal nothing from this place except its memories, whatever they turned out to be.

The note then, lying on the parquet floor beneath the flap of the front door. Just one folded piece of paper.

William, he read, however difficult, we have to talk. Call me. 087 4736593.

How odd, he thought, as he slipped the note into his pocket, lifted the post-flap to see the coast outside was clear and opened the latch on the front door. How odd that he didn't have her number.

24

He would have to wean himself off her, Jeremy told him. In the series of low stone rooms by the inlet of the river, William and Jeremy, intermittent associates, never quite friends. He observed Jeremy's head, as he bent over the drinks cabinet by the long, too-modern plate glass window with the reflections of the evening sun dying on the water outside.

"The way you weaned yourself off Susannah."

"Divorce managed that," William replied. "It was a marriage, and a ridiculous one—"

"But the situation is surely exploitative, unless you enjoy it. Someone enters your life, under false pretences, begins a relationship, without any disclosure of—"

"She didn't begin it. I began it."

"Why did she keep secret the thing she knew?"

"Embarrassment?"

"Whatever. It stinks, my man—"

"The way the moss did."

"Moss?"

"The moss from the well."

"I thought it was the water."

"The moss. She made a paste from it. It cured my hands."

"And you believed all that?"

"Here is the evidence."

He held them out. His hands. And Jeremy turned to the plate glass window, the dying sun on the inlet outside. His scepticism didn't need expression.

"There are all sorts of reasons, my dear William, to have someone in your life. A lie should not be one of them."

"Who lied to whom?"

"I'm talking about a lie of omission. Full disclosure."

"Were you taught by the Jesuits, Jeremy?"

"No. But I have a Jesuitical cast of mind. You remember your *Desert Island Discs?*"

"No. But you obviously do."

"I never quite believed your choices. Bob Marley, Thelonious Monk. Ella Fitzgerald. 'Manhattan'."

"Rodgers and Hart," William said. "Don't knock show tunes. And that one has a Schubertian simplicity—"

"You have this almost pathological fear that your audience won't like you. I know what your tastes were. Mahler. Schönberg. Strauss – and not the Viennese one. But yet, here you were, pretending to be hip—"

"You saw right through me?"

"And maybe she does too."

So, he would have to wean himself off her, he thought, as he was driving back. Give himself simple tasks, like an addict in a rehab clinic. Cleaning the kitchen floor. Scouring the fridge. Smoothing the bed sheets.

And he began these simple tasks the next day, trying to keep the piano out of his gaze, since the thought of playing without her would somehow break his heart. But every facet of the house just reminded him of her. Will I have to leave this place too, he wondered, and returned to what seemed to have become his only recourse, the Jaguar.

He drove down the main street, slowly, past the empty wooden benches outside Mary's coffee shop, and wondered how this street, this nondescript village and townland, could exist without her. He would have driven past her house, if he'd known where she lived, and he realized he didn't even have her phone number. He could sit here, parked, for hours, until she appeared, or even work up the courage to place another notice in Mary's shop. Wanted. To the one who used to be my housekeeper.

He felt foolish then, as the lunchtime bustle began to gather in the street, and drove down towards the small harbour, where he could at least park and observe whatever footfall happened on the distant beach. And that's where he saw her walking, towards the thin band of froth that was the retreating tide. There was a line of some kind, with fish hanging from it. She stopped there and waited, as by some arrangement. And then he saw with whom. A man, tallish, thin, walking from the untidy edge of trees onto the rocky stones of the foreshore, with a bucket in his hand.

25

She took a sleeping pill around four in the morning and woke when the sun was flooding over her bedroom floor. She checked her phone to see had William rung, felt an empty breath soughing from her when she realized that would have been a first, as up to then he hadn't had her number. But she saw that it was nearing twelve. She had a strange impulse then that she followed, without questioning. She checked the tides.

She saw that high tide had passed five hours ago and that low tide was approaching. Those nightlines only revealed their catch, she knew, when the tide retreated. So she knew where to find the other one and probably when.

She had the strangest image, of a horned fish like a narwhal hanging off one of his hooks. What a narwhal was she had no idea, beyond the fact that it was a fish and had some kind of magical horn. She could feel the tide retreating as she dressed, a sun-dappled ceiling descending slowly towards the dangling hooks and whatever the hooks had caught. She tucked her tracksuit bottoms into a pair of wellington boots since she knew how damp the sand could be, walked out through her back door, over the low garden wall and into the tangle of trees that separated it from the foreshore. She had to stop herself from running. What was this absurd fear that she would miss the moment of an encounter she didn't even want but knew she had to have? But the trees gave way to the stony grass that led to the white sand, and beyond it the wet brown sand and beyond that again the endless tide. It took her ten minutes to reach the water's edge, and another twenty along the runnels and flurries of retreating water to where the same arrangement of rods, lines and hooks was already poking through the water.

There was nobody to view it but her, so she turned and squinted her eyes against the bright sunlight where the ragged line of trees led back towards her cottage. It had no substance, could hardly be called a forest, but there must be a word for it, a copse, maybe, and then she saw the pale blue caravan deep amongst them and knew that's where he had made his bed. Like some kind of migrant animal, she thought, finding transitory shelter, and she wondered how transitory it would turn out to be.

She had to have this conversation. The well had provided her with some respite, but could make no reply. And then she saw the caravan door open and the thin, pencil-like figure move through the trees. He had a bucket in his hand, of course. If there was anywhere to meet him, it was here. The winds were still cold and only the very lonely walked this stretch of beach. She sensed the fish giving a last gasp of life behind her and wondered was this how he planned to survive here. She could get him work on the trawlers, if fishing was his thing. They could meet every ten days or so on his return, out in Castletownbere, maybe, far from prying eyes. So nobody would remark on her revulsion. She had always wondered how she would respond to this event, if it was to happen. What she could never have anticipated was the distaste she felt, for this tall, rather rancid-smelling youth in collapsing trainers. She had anticipated guilt, a rush of confused emotion, a period of overwhelming overcompensation for whatever she had abandoned. But all she felt was a cold, and rather visceral, dislike. She remembered the unattractive youths that would insist on pawing her round various dancefloors and remembered the same quiet, cold and helpless fury. She would have kneed them in the bulging crotch, if her body had responded to what her emotions were telling her. How could you hate your own flesh and blood? But she for some reason did, now that she had encountered it.

And now he was close to her and she could hear the swinging bucket and the squelching of his trainers off the soft sand.

"Here again," he said.

"We could make it a habit."

"A habit?"

"When the tide's out and your nightline's full. I see the fish flapping and know that you're there."

She looked back towards the harbour. The retreating tide.

"Here—"

"Only mackerel today," he said. "They must have been running."

He began to strip them, bloodily, from the hooks and drop them in the bucket.

"You like mackerel?"

"Not a fish person, really."

"No?"

"You have to tell me why," she said.

"You must have known it would happen, someday."

"I suppose I always did. So why now?"

"I had a habit," he said.

"A habit?"

"A drug habit."

163

He hit his elbow with a dead mackerel, leaving blood on the sleeve.

"And now I'm clean. The advice was—"

"Advice from whom?"

"Therapist."

There must have been a therapist, he reasoned. Her Alastair was the kind that never stopped talking. He remembered the soliloquies carried away on the wind-shaken scaffold, painting the orange on the storage tanks.

"In Stanley's Well."

And that name came, quite easily.

"Stanley's Well?"

"The rehab place. They told me – to find out all the hidden things. And face them."

Then he turned to face her. He had another fish in his hand, still alive and flapping.

He managed a smile.

She didn't. And he had to wonder, once more, why he was doing this. It was an obscure kind of revenge, he knew. But whose revenge?

But it was true. All the rehab places said the same. He wondered where the nearest one was now. He could feel the urge.

"So you wanted to face me?"

"Yes," he nodded.

"And now that you have, what do you feel?"

"Me? I feel what I've always felt. Lonely."

And he was surprised at how easy it was. A lie never works, he had always known, unless it has a kernel of truth. He had been an addict, probably still was, if the therapists he had spoken to were to be given any credence. There had been no Stanley's Well, but the name could have fitted any of the drab premises he had been sent to. The situation demanded these lies or half-truths. This woman on the damp strand, whose attractions, he had to admit to himself, were still evident, drew them effortlessly out of him. She needed them, and he didn't mind being needed.

"I came to finish something," he said.

"To finish what?"

"Whatever the rehab told me."

"What was that?"

"You have to face them."

"Face what?"

"Your demons."

He could see that statement upset her. He could see a large cloud heading towards them, over the sea which was flat no longer, suddenly whipped into multiple fringes of white.

"And I'm your demon?"

"Dunno. Are you?"

And he wondered then, could he draw her out. What was the story with that mansion, and the scribbled note and the grand piano? Was it something to do with theirs? Their story? And again, he was surprised at how easy it was.

"There's a word," he said. "And I'm afraid to say it."

"You're not good with words?"

"No."

"Then don't say it."

He couldn't. It would be too much.

"I don't want to use again—"

He could see the effect that had on her. She reached out and touched his arm, bloodied with the mackerel.

"Mother—"

He allowed himself to slump towards her, and the feeling was real. He didn't want to use again. And a mother surely would have helped. He was aware of her hand, and its attempt to press his head towards her shoulder.

She tried to manage her feeling of revulsion, but didn't succeed. It must have shown, she realized, in the teeth clamped on her lower lip, the tears trying to force their way out of her blinking eyelashes. She turned away to hide these things and he slumped towards her again. And she felt his bony knees, thighs and hips crunch against hers. It seemed impossible that she'd given birth to this lean, dishevelled thing, stinking of dead mackerel and unwashed denim. But she had.

And the rain was on them, suddenly. It was a blessed relief. The water running down her face, instead of tears, the fresh, metallic smell. How could that bath of hazy drops feel so welcome on her skin? She lived in the country of the rain, after all. It allowed her to slip from his grasp, step back, until he was almost lost in wet, misty haze.

"You want some mackerel?" he asked, through the downpour.

"Not today," she said, and suddenly felt stupid.

"My gift. You gave me me. I give you fish."

"Is that a fair return?"

"God only knows."

Why did he have to bring god into it? Maybe that was one push too far. But he couldn't tell if she minded, one step away from him, in a waterfall all of her own.

William watched it all on the wet pier, from the watery windscreen, behind the rhythmic soughing of the wipers. Jealousy was a new emotion, and he considered this stranger as it did its work on him. A quickening of the breath, a pain beneath his ribcage which reminded him that he had, after all, a heart, and it was now suffering the banal indignity of being broken. He thought of all of the melodies, all of the ridiculous show tunes that referenced the same event and was amazed at how accurate they were to the sensation he was now feeling. He had known for some time now that he needed her. He had thought that need was a form of weakness, an indignity even, not so much to him as to her. But that he loved her the way the popular songs implied was a new realization and it came to him, like all emotional things, too late to be of any use whatsoever. He had been captured by a curtain of clichés, a red velvet drape that pulled back to reveal a soda fountain, on a cheap Broadway set. What were their names? Rodgers and Hart. He thought of that odd, perfect rhyme, wondering what street compares with Mott Street. When was it, June or July?

But there it was. He would never take her to Mott Street in Manhattan and his heart was broken.

He turned the key and the engine coughed itself to life. He could see a shape, in the torrent of falling drops, walking back towards the harbour and he knew it was her. He reversed the car in the rain, could have fallen in the brine below, such was his hurry, such was the fury of the rainstorm that occluded his vision. He wondered would she recognize the car, if she could even see it through the torrent, and he was anxious not to add to his current set of indignities. But she must be drenched, he thought, and if she was, how ungentlemanly of him not to offer her a lift. Maybe if he did, it would help his case. But the road was snaking towards him, out of the gathering rain, and as he continued down it he wondered what that case could be.

She had every right to find an alternative. Or to have an alternative, which maybe had been her way all along. One that young, even, and he had no idea of her companion's age, given the occlusion of the rainstorm, but he had to be younger than William Barrow. The William Barrow that had met her three times, and each time assumed he was meeting a different person. She had kept her memories to herself. He could understand the logic, but the reasons, no. And perhaps she had been a different person each time. Only he remained frozen in – what was her term – his boundless narcissism, his devotion to perfection on that set of ivory keys. While she changed, he stayed the same. And yet again, the woman he saw in the driving rain was a different creature to the one who had listened to his Shostakovich and recognized the same failure. Maybe that was his fate, to stay the frozen, self-regarding same. He had always taken a bitter kind of joy in his capacity for isolation. Very few people could do it. Could bear this life, hotel room after hotel room, airport lounges, the watery applause of his ageing audience, the warm white wine afterwards. But now, when the elm and poplar trees appeared between the half-circle of the windscreen wipers, in the driving rain, the same isolation had become like a stench he could no longer bear. The cloud of a foreign presence around him, like the stale cigarette smoke of a hated familiar. He wondered could he get through the night alone.

He tried to spend the time playing, with the fingers that she had healed. And his Brahms and his Chopin couldn't rise to this occasion. Only the same show tune came to mind – 'Manhattan' – picked out in stiff classical style.

He would have thought Schubert's *Nacht und Träume* would approximate more to what he was feeling. But no, there was no grandeur to this feeling. It was as simple and as immediate as pain.

He took a sleeping pill in the early morning. It gave him three hours of comparative oblivion, and he awoke to the relentless knocking of the front door. He pulled his clothes on while the knocking continued, thinking it couldn't be her. She had her own key, after all. And any return of her into his life was too much to hope for.

26

She had recognized the car, of course. And she knew, by its rather guilty retreat from the sodden pier, what its presence meant. She felt guilty herself when she woke the next morning. Not for any womb-ripped, Oedipal reasons, but for the simple fact that she had told him the truth, but not the whole truth. So she cycled back up there, and the rain had left its residue everywhere. In the small runnel down the main street, in the overgrown grasses that licked her ankles, in the overhanging April boughs that branched over her, beyond the rectory entrance. She cycled up again, in her red raincoat again, and knocked on the mottled glass again.

And he opened the door again, after the smallest of pauses, which let her know he had been waiting for her.

"Was that your car," she asked, "in the rain, by the pier?"

"It was, I'm embarrassed to say," he admitted. "It's a new emotion for me."

"Embarrassment?" she asked, and couldn't help but smile.

"No," he said. And his answering smile was more of a grimace. "Jealousy."

"Jealousy? Whatever for?"

"Well, we didn't leave on the best of terms. And I saw you there, in the rain, with—"

How strange, she thought. And there was another thought below it. How delightful, how adolescent.

She smiled.

"Your rival?"

And she said it.

"How strange. And how kind of adolescent."

"As I said, it's a new emotion for me."

"You want to be young again?"

And he grimaced back.

"Not if that's what it means—"

She came close to him. Curled her fingers into his. And how really strange now, she thought. They could have been two teenagers.

"There's no need for that," she said. "I wasn't meeting your replacement."

"No?"

She took a breath.

"I was meeting your son."

And the strangest thing was, as he would tell her much later, that he felt neither anger nor confusion. His only feeling was of a kind of delicious relief.

"My son?" he asked.

"Our son. So he claims. I had a child, after that episode in Brighton. I should have told you."

"When?"

"When should I have told you? When I took this job, maybe. When we got... together..."

The word felt odd in her mouth. She wasn't a teenager, she thought.

"And what?"

"The usual. Irish story. Abortion or adoption. I chose the latter. And he's hunted me down."

She gave a bitter little smile. So unlike her, he thought. And then the further thought: what did he really know of her?

"Us down."

Will nothing behave in this story of ours, he wondered? And he did say ours to himself, not mine. Or hers.

He led her inside by the hand. He sat her down, made her a cup of tea. And he became an adult again.

"Aren't there procedures," he asked her, "in cases like this? Doesn't one get notice, from adoption agencies and the like?"

"There had been a request for contact," she told him, "which I hadn't replied to. So someone must have put two and two together."

"His adoptive parents?"

She shrugged.

"He is not beyond it, himself."

"Are you in shock?"

"Are you?"

"I'm in a state that I have no words for," he said.

"Join the club."

"You seem afraid of him."

"Maybe I am," she said. "Someone was in my house. I found a letter on the floor."

She took it from her pocket and unfolded it.

"He broke in?"

"Maybe the door was left open."

"Is he a threat?"

"Isn't everyone at that age? Though you probably wouldn't know."

"I wouldn't?"

"Not being a woman. The ones hanging outside the chipper. The pub after closing. Always young men. Young men in jeans and trainers. His needed cleaning. He probably sleeps in the woods behind."

"Behind?"

"Behind the beach."

"Perhaps you just need to get to know each other."

"Do I?"

There were tears now, coursing down her face.

"Do you?"

He remembered his own mother. The sound of the door slamming, in Richmond.

"Children need to be loved."

"He's not a child," she said. "And what do you know about love?"

"Ouch," he said.

"I'm sorry. I could ask the same of myself."

"I'm learning," he said. "I'm learning all of the sentimental lessons."

He reached out and tried to wipe her face dry.

"It's a bit late, I know. For both of us."

"I could take you to Manhattan," he said.

She brushed his hand away from her cheek.

"I need you to make sense," she said.

"But maybe it would make sense. To get away from all of this. We could find out what street compares with Mott Street in July?"

"It's not July now. It's April."

"April in Manhattan then. There must be a song for that."

"Paris," she said.

173

"Paris?"

"'April in Paris'. I used to play it on the cruise ship."

"You played on a cruise ship?"

"The captain's wife had a thing about singing it."

He tried to imagine the captain's wife. And a cruise ship, inching round some moonlit bay. He failed.

"I know so little about you."

"Well, now you know more."

And when he didn't reply, she went.

27

He had been dreaming unfamiliar dreams. At first he thought it was the withdrawal which drained all the colour from them. Whatever freshness had been in his dreams had vanished, in some interregnum between leaving one caravan and arriving in another. And then, that night, with the wind beating against the unfamiliar window which would never really properly open or close, he realized what it was. He was dreaming someone else's dreams. And they could only be Alastair's.

He knew he had pushed it too far then, and like a crab scurrying home to the ocean, he felt like pulling it backwards. Why was he doing this, what had he got to gain, some sense of guilt or obscure revenge for the dead Alastair he had left on the damp mattress back in Cleethorpes? He tried the card for one last time in the SuperValu, and was almost relieved when it was declined. So it was over, he thought, time to forget this little skit and get back to the serious business of wandering. There were fishing boats needing hands in the nearby peninsula, he could hitch a ride there, or even walk if it came to that, and he lit a small fire by the blue caravan and wondered would caravans be his only dwellings in whatever future presented itself to him. He deserved more than a collapsing caravan. He thought of her sweet cottage in the back laneway and of the big house down through the avenue of trees and wondered again what the story was there. He scraped the skin and gutted two of the mackerel, set a pan from the collapsing kitchen and smoked, while he waited for the pan to heat. Then he heard the footsteps, the crackling tread coming through the brambles, and he thought they must be hers. The footsteps sounded heavier, though, and he had a moment of panic, while he watched the mackerel flesh brown. Had she told the old bill, the fuzz, the polis, or whatever they were called here? The guards, he remembered.

And a figure came through the holly and ash trees, a tall figure, dressed in an open gabardine coat, with greying hair and long thin fingers.

"What do you want?" this figure asked. "Money?"

The accent was English. Posh, as well. Had those tones the news used to be read in.

"Money," he replied, "always comes in handy."

And he thought then, it must be him. He pictured the immensity of the dark piano against the living room window. That smell of polished floorboards. Wealth.

"There are ways," this one said, "to approach one's adoptive parents. Procedures. I can't for the life of me understand why you didn't avail of them."

The shoes. Stitched leather, too good for the mud that stained them. And above them, oddly, mismatched socks.

"There was the letter," he replied, thinking, how deep does this get? And he knew then he was going to push it further. Until, and fuck it, he thought, the bough did break. And down would come baby and cradle and all.

"You broke into her house," this one said.

And yours, he thought. Such a difference between them. Different pianos. What was that about?

"The back door was open," he said. "It was a kind of invite."

And it was, he thought. The key, underneath the pot by the mat.

"So you just walked in?"

"I wanted to see the house her Alastair could have grown up in."

"And that's your name? Alastair?"

He let that one lie there. He didn't even nod. And he was amazed again at how easy it was for a lie to pull bits of the truth around it, grow itself into a tangled forest.

"So you left the letter?"

"I dropped it."

And this at least was true.

"But you must have wanted her to know."

"That the one she abandoned had turned up."

"So I can only ask you again, what is it you want? Money?"

Money would come in handy, he thought. And this elegant one, in the gabardine coat, reeked of it. Might as well go all in.

"Maybe. Or maybe the thing money can't buy. You know the song."

"The song?"

"Your generation. The Beatles. Can't buy me love."

And this elicited a reaction, he was pleased to see. Even a possible tear. The other took a handkerchief from his top pocket and dabbed those grey eyes.

"I didn't abandon you."

Aha. So here was the heart of the thing.

"No?"

"I didn't know. That she had had a child."

So, there was another story here. And of course, he wanted to know more.

177

"But you know now."

"Yes. I know everything now. But you can imagine how difficult it must be for her."

And the grey eyes met his own. Were his own eyes grey? Kind of. Grey, green.

"No, I take that back. You can't. You could never. So if you want to give it some thought, call me at the rectory."

"The rectory?"

He didn't need directions. Already knew where it was.

"Yes. On the Bantry Road. If you want to..."

Tears again. The handkerchief, doing its business.

"... resolve these issues..."

He watched him walk back through the tangled wood. And he thought, yes, it might be interesting, even fun to resolve these issues. Alastair did deserve some resolution.

28

When we don't know what to do we walk, she thought to herself. And if that was the case she could be walking for the rest of her inconsequential life. She walked down Main Street to Mary's but couldn't bring herself to go in and have a coffee and face the prospect of whatever conversation that might entail. She saw the benches crowded with April day trippers and realized summer would soon be here. She walked past them, and the waft of cigarette smoke and fresh, bitter coffee, down towards the harbour where she was met by the nauseous odour of fish. There were nets drying on the small harbour wall and Peter's was not amongst the boats moored there. She walked back towards the town, and followed the Cork Road and the row of grey granite houses towards the end and realized the police station was at the end of them, and wondered had some protective instinct led her there. Her house had been burgled, after all, and she still had the letter in her pocket. But what does she report? My abandoned son broke into my home. What should have been his home? Then she saw the cracked window of the station and the note affixed to the inside referring all enquiries to Bantry, and remembered that the Orran station had been closed for a year now. So she was saved the confusion of that encounter. She took a note of the Bantry number on her phone in case she ever needed it. Then she couldn't face the return journey through the town so she turned left at the harbour, to trace a path through the trees back to her cottage. She avoided the beach and the prospect of another encounter when she saw the blue peeling caravan set in its little copse of ash and realized she had been led like a homing pigeon to his transitory dwelling.

There was a plastic chair, the two back legs of which were bent and half buried in the drying mud. There were the two metal staves of the nightlines, the tendrils of hooks and catgut wafting between them. There were the dusty remnants of a fire, cold burnt wood and an array of fish bones scattered about which she felt she should warn him about, since they could attract rats and cats. But he wasn't there, she could tell, there was a silence about the caravan that was absolute, somehow, the only sound being the distant fall of the ocean and the buzzing of insects. Summer was almost here, she realized, and whoever owned this caravan would come to reclaim it and she wondered what kind of business that would entail, the flashing lights of the Bantry police car through the trees, the claim of some kind of consanguinity to the piano teacher in the cottage, or even the pianist in the rectory on the Bantry Road. But he had only traced her, she remembered, not his putative father and then she had a flash of panic, realizing how easy that could have been. Any enquiry round the town, a word dropped by Mary Culleton, and even without those, it dawned on her how criminally easy she would have been to follow. He had followed her home, after all, or had he traced her cottage through the address on the letter? She wondered then what kind of pleasure the transgression afforded him, the so badly concealed key by the potted plant, the quiet entry through the back door. And she pushed at the sagging mildewed blue door of the caravan and it wouldn't give, of course, they never open inwards. So she pulled, and it came away with a sudden jerk, almost fell off its hinges, which wouldn't do at all, she realized, she must be cleverer than him and leave no evidence of her presence.

There. Inside the caravan, the sun hitting the damp piece of carpet or was it linoleum covering the unsteady floor. There was a small pull-out table, with an overflowing ashtray, the only other evidence of an inhabitant being the unwashed dishes in the metal sink. She turned the taps on, and was happy to see the water was at least flowing, and had to resist the urge to begin cleaning the scum of the plate, the browning cup. She must leave no evidence, she reminded herself, despite her revulsion at the thought of a child of her own living like this. The bed against the back window with the ruffled sleeping bag. She gently lifted it and saw another sleeping bag beneath it, one brown, one blue. He must be cold at night, she thought, but summer's coming, he won't have to freeze for that much longer. And the only other evidence of his presence was a credit card, lying on the linoleum beneath the bed, bent in two to make it useless. He must have run out of money, she thought, and again the nurturing instinct took over and she wondered how and where he could continue to live. She brought the card to the beam of sunlight and didn't dare to uncrush it, but read his name on the dark plastic.

Mr Alastair J Hitchens. Expires end of 04/22.

And she wondered what the J stood for. Alastair John. Alastair James. Alastair Joshua.

She would have preferred the Joshua, she thought, placing the card where she had found it.

29

William could see a hulking shape behind the mottled glass. And when he had managed the open door, the same youth in what they called a hoodie, with the same muddy trainers and a bucket in his hand.

"I brought you these," this overgrown child said.

He proffered the bucket. William could see grey water inside, disturbed by the flapping of fish.

"Why?"

A scaled tail flipped in the sloshing water.

"Caught them by the shore. Thought I had to bring sommat."

"So you've come to resolve these issues?"

"You said you didn't know."

"Know what?"

"That you had a kid."

"She did tell me, eventually."

"Whatdoyoucallher. Tara."

And William felt a frisson of anger at the use of her name. Why, he couldn't quite understand. What does any son call a mother?

"Glad she did. Otherwise this would be more awkward than it already is."

It was more than awkward. But William couldn't find the word for it.

"And here. These are for you."

He proffered the bucket again. Edged past William, inside, leaving an odour, of sweat and tobacco. And of something sweeter, harder to define. Like mulch.

Transgressive, William thought. Those muddy trainers were transgressing.

"You have any old newspaper? Or a plastic bag?"

He walked past the piano, into the kitchen. He made himself instantly at home.

"Like this."

He took a SuperValu shopping bag from the counter. Took the still flapping fish from the bucket, with greasy hands, and dumped them inside.

"You have a freezer?"

William said nothing.

"Don't know what you have, do you?"

He crossed the flagstones, pulled open the bottom door of the fridge.

"Here."

He placed the rolled bag inside the freezer.

"Keep forever they will. Cook her a nice meal, whenever she comes back."

If she comes back, William thought. And as if the transgressor had divined his thoughts, he asked:

"Would your bairn have grown up here..."

He pushed the scullery door open.

"Or in her gaff?"

"What do you know about us?"

"Separate houses. There's been a whatdoyoucallit…"

He bent both hands, as if splitting a twig.

"… a rupture. But a bairn still needs looking after. Even one that turns up this late."

He pushed the scullery door open.

"Nice gaff," he said. "A pity Alastair couldn't enjoy it."

"Alastair?"

"Me. Your boy. Her bairn."

He trundled down the steps, outside. And William felt he had to follow.

"What do we have here? A garden. An orchard. A trellis thingy."

He made his way through it. Again, William followed. Through the trellis, where William had to grab his shirt, hold him back.

"A hole in the ground?"

"A well," said William.

"Well, well. A well."

He stared down at the dark tube of nothingness. Then turned, to find William behind him.

"We're the same size, you and me."

"We are, I suppose."

"So I suppose you could say, I've adapted myself."

"You mean adopted?"

"No. I mean adapted. Myself. To my situation. Which has been, throughout my short, pathetic life, adoption."

"And your adoptive parents?"

"Fuck them. I have you two now."

"You've shared this with her?"

"The mum? Does she share much? Seems she doesn't like him much."

"Him?"

"Her Alastair. Me."

"You gave her reason."

"Suppose I did?"

"You can understand the shock."

"Been waiting, I suppose. For the ghost to turn up. The ghost from the past. You can't abandon someone without consequences."

"No?"

"No. Life doesn't work like that."

"What do you know about life, Alastair?"

"I do know that."

And he raised his face to William's and smiled.

"You used my name. That's sweet."

He walked to the edge of the well and peered down.

"Kind of dangerous, isn't it? Hole in the ground, falling away like that? So deep."

"There's a history to it."

"Aha. One of those kinds of wells. Then it deserves something more than this crappy trellis thingy. A whatdoyoucall it. Grotto. With shells and things. We could do it together."

"We could?"

"Father-son kind of thing. What's the word? Bonding."

There was a pile of sand and a smaller pile of cement at the edge of the bed of nettles. He ran his fingers through the sand, and turned to William and smiled. And William allowed himself to think how, with a little grooming, he could look presentable. Even attractive.

"You're not good at the old cement and mortar, I would hazard a guess. But you can leave that to me. That and the shells."

30

The days were lengthening and the April sunlight was generally warming the ground under her feet. Everything but her own mood, she realized, and she thought a swim might help. Clear the fog out of which every thought of hers seemed to blunder.

Could you hate your own flesh and blood?
    She was wondering that as the cold water lapped her ankles.
    Fruit of your womb?
    She plunged herself down and felt the cold rip through her.

And there is my fruit, my issue, my progeny, she thought when she emerged, the water dripping from the bleached and overstretched bathing suit designed for eyes other than his and for bodies other than what hers had become. And even though he was silhouetted by the sun behind him, she could feel his sly almost smile, when he raised himself upwards from whatever he was gathering from the shingle round the waterline. He was collecting something. Shellfish, she thought, seeing the bulging supermarket bags by his side. No, she thought, when he moved towards her and she heard the bags rattle and scrape. Shells, nothing more.

"Brave lady," he said. "Swimming."

"And you're foraging?"

"Is that what it's called?" he replied, in that guttural growl.

"Cockles, mussels? Razor clams?"

She had heard there were whole Internet clubs devoted to the practice.

"Just the shells," he told her. "For the grotto."

"The grotto?"

"Didn't he tell you?"

"Didn't who tell me?"

"William."

"We haven't spoken."

"Aha. Hope I had nothing to do with it."

"You did, a little."

"Well, I'm building him a grotto."

She let that lie. She hoped she had heard it wrong.

"For that well of his."

Mine, she thought. It is nothing if not my well. And she knew, somewhere inside her, some battle had begun.

"And what's the grotto?"

"Around the well. Just an idea. But, if we ever get round to it, we will need seashells. Scallop, clam, barnacle. Whatever. Need shells for a grotto, don't you?"

"I suppose you do."

"And it's a hazard. Being just there, a hole in the ground. So I proposed a kind of grotto, like in all the holy places."

"Holy places?"

"You know what I mean."

"You're religious?"

"Just kind of... spiritual..."

"And a grotto needs shells?"

"Come to the caravan, I'll show you my design."

So she towelled herself in the cold wind behind the dunes and dressed and descended the dunes to meet him, and he walked her through the sand to the stony border and forest of diminutive trees beyond.

She knew where it was, but let him lead her towards it. The same faded blue caravan, sitting amongst the broken ash and holly trees, the ragwort and dock leaves.

"It was sitting empty," he said by way of explanation and pulled open the half-hanging door, told her to make herself at home on the broken chair by the steps and went inside. So she sat, gingerly, amongst the buzzing bluebottles and the smell of sweet mulch. He came out two minutes later, smelling of much the same, with a brown paper bag in his hand, which he spread, squatting beside her, on his thin knees.

"Used to walk past one of them on my way to school."

"In Hull?"

"But they all would have statues inside them. Don't need a statue, do we?"

"You said you're spiritual—"

"But not religious."

He had drawn a semi-circular wall around an outlined circle of black, rising into an oval shape above. There was a childish intensity to the drawing which made her feel something. What it was, she wasn't sure.

"The well's the thing," he said. "Doesn't need no statue."

It was fear, she realized, when he stood up again in one supple movement. He had the body of an athlete, the point of view of a child. She should have felt empathy, warmth, even love, but all she felt was a shiver of apprehension.

He stretched down a hand. She had no option but to take it.

"Come on," he said. "Let's scope it out together."

"Scope?" she asked.

"The well. Your William."

He pulled her from the broken chair, legs still stuck in the mud, to her feet. Again, one easy movement, with no apparent effort. She could feel his strength, even from the single hand that gripped hers.

"This."

He folded the brown paper bag carefully, as if it was a parchment.

The walk, then back to her bike, hidden amongst the dunes, along the beach to the back road.

"Your bike needs oil," he said, after yet another random squeak from the wheel.

"It does," she said, and she wondered was there a word for the stretches of silence between them. It wasn't companionable.

"I could get my hands on a can."

"No need," she said.

"But there is," he said. "There is definitely a need. Show me here."

And he took the bike from her hands, spun it in the air like a child's toy, delivered a deft kick to the back wheel, and set it down again.

"There," he said, wheeling it backwards and forwards. She took it and resumed her trudge towards the rectory.

He followed.

"No squeak," he said.

"Thank you," she replied.

"But it still needs oil."

"You're handy," she said, when she used the bike's front wheel to push open the gate.

"Always have been. Wonder where I got that from."

She could see William by the portico, one hand on the door handle. She wondered had they been expected.

"Probably from him."

It was odd, watching him push past William and make his way into the interior. She felt the sense of a new emotion. She remembered what William had said about jealousy and how it surprised him. And when William with that diffident courtesy of his offered to make some tea, she found a word for it. Infringement.

She felt infringed, usurped, transgressed, even though the interior wasn't hers.

She asked could she use the loo and made her way upstairs. And everything smelt of...

She could find no word for it but "him". Everything smelt of him.

She scoured the sink free of the butt ends of rolled-up cigarettes.

She came back down to William pouring the tea and the thick phlegmy burr elaborating on how the grotto should be a semi-circular one, piece of cake as construction, the hard surface of the concrete inlaid with seashells.

"Are you up for this, William?"

It was the first time she'd used his name in some time.

"Oh, William is," the other answered. "William is all for it. I'll keep the costs down."

"The costs?"

"No need to spend a fortune. Cement, sand, a mixer. The shells are free."

She turned her face from him to William.

"I asked your—"

She found it remarkably hard to get the word out.

"—father."

"The thing is a hazard," William said. "You must admit. Sitting out there, amongst the crab apples."

"The orchard," she said softly. And as she sipped her tea, she felt something else, stronger than transgression. Something dark and infinite, deeper than the well.

31

Was he moving in? It was hard to tell. He filled one sleeping bag with shells, the old and tatty blue one, and carried the other one rolled under his muscled arm as he made his way through the saplings that seemed to want to be trees. A bit like himself, he thought, a stray who wanted to be a son. But they bent in the breeze and gave way to his thrusting shoulders, gently. For some reason he kept under the leaf cover, and when it came to the main road, he waited until the last car had scudded by before he made his own rapid crossing.

Maybe Alastair was moving in. Again it was hard to tell. But one thing was clear, Alastair had something criminal in mind. The few small thefts executed in the almost comically unguarded mansion hardly qualified as thefts. A twenty euro note here and there, it kept him going. But was there something bigger looming? A rough going over on that old piano man, until he disclosed where the real treasure was hidden. And there was treasure, there had to be, a safe in an upstairs room or attic that he hadn't yet found. He remembered the dead one's fancy that his mother dwelt in realms of gold. Again, the innocent had got that one half right. It wasn't the mother, it was the father. But if Alastair was planning a crime, he hadn't shared the details with him yet. But he must have been planning something, hence the scurry over the empty road, the quick scramble over the brick wall. He didn't want to be observed. Yet.

He had unrolled the second sleeping bag in a garden shed the first night. The hardened mud floor was not as comfortable as the caravan, but at least it provided the perfect cloak of alone-ness. He didn't want company, he didn't want prying eyes. He didn't want trouble, of any kind, but he kind of knew trouble was coming.

There was a sadness to being someone else, he realized. Even your dreams weren't your own. It began to anger him as he lay there, on the hardened mud ground with the smell of woodchip and fertilizer all around him. He had not, after all, constructed this little story. They themselves had; he had just happened into whatever game they had played between them and maybe it was time to bring that game to its conclusion.

But what would the conclusion be? Again, hard to tell. It was easier to deal with the father than the mother, that had become abundantly and immediately clear to him. Whatever cement he was trowelling and ladling round the trellis could have had the opposite effect to a protective one, could have tripped someone so easily and sent them tumbling down below. But he didn't want any tumbling. Not yet. He could hear the piano playing in the evening light as he pressed in another scallop or cockle shell into the wet beginnings of a grotto and then washed his hands in the bucket, and thought to himself, fuck the hard ground and the garden shed, Alastair deserves better. So he gathered his good sleeping bag from the shed and made his way through the scullery. He laid it out over the couch in the wide living room and saw no hint of enquiry from the ersatz father tinkling the keys. Much easier to deal with than her.

"Nice number," he said, as he rolled himself one.

NEIL JORDAN

"Indeed," came the reply. And that would do, for now. Later he could scurry in through the scullery, fillet out any cans of lager or half-emptied bottles of port. That indeed would do fine, for this night.

32

There was a circular lip of dried cement with cockle shells protruding from some of the surfaces. So this was the grotto, she surmised, walking round it with her Cuban-heeled boots, tracing the squashed cigarette butts, wondering where the entrance, if it was ever to be finished, would be. Maybe entrances didn't concern him. Maybe the grotto was to keep others out, not invite them in.

But when she made her way through the kitchen door, she knew he already inhabited it. William was filling the kettle but whatever scent was in the air wasn't his. It smelt of mulch, decaying bark, old tobacco.

She hated asking, but felt she had to. Would he still need a cleaner? He told her he would be lost without one. So she arranged to come by, every second day, determined to outlast this new arrangement of things. She saw minimal progress on the plans for the grotto, but the sense of him inside the rectory grew, even when he wasn't there. She found rolled cigarette butts in the window sills, lager cans on the toilet floor, shaven hairs in the sink.

She found a burnt foil in the bathroom and had decided to resign herself to whatever contract was between them now, when she saw the bruise on William's left cheek.

"What happened?" she asked, knowing already his reply would be an untruth.

"A fall," he said, as she pulled a wad of cotton from the medicine cabinet and dabbed it with iodine.

"Where did you fall?"

"By the well," he said.

"You're lying," she said.

"I am," he said. "It's a new emotion for me. Shame. Along with jealousy."

"He hit you."

"He did," William said.

"Where?"

"By the well. But I swung at him first. Is that the way it is? Between fathers and sons?"

"Tell me."

And he told her.

It was the butt of the rollie stuck between the piano keys. Between the A and the B flat, William found the keys jammed and extracted it with the help of a toothpick, and confronted the transgressor as he was doing press-ups by the crab apple tree, another rollie stuck in his mouth. The argument flared, don't get your knickers in a twist about it old man, and maybe it was the smile that did it, rather than the innuendo. Let herself clean it up.

William, whose hands had never clenched into a fist before, found the nails biting into the palms and his forearm punching forwards like a piston towards that smiling face. The face ducked, of course, had long seen the danger coming and a right-hand haymaker came back. It caught William just below the left eye and sent him sailing through the air, and if the other hadn't caught him, ripping three or four shirt buttons in the act, he could have tumbled into that dark green telescope below him.

"Sorry," the tall skinny one said in his workaday burr. "But next time, don't signal it so blatantly. We dunnae want you falling in, do we?"

The tattooed hand pulled William back from the grassy precipice.

"Come in now, I'll look after that bruise."

But he didn't. She did.

"You've heard of elder abuse?" she asked, as she dabbed the broken capillaries around his cheek. "You'll have to ask him to go."

"I can't," he said. "And if you're honest, neither can you."

How could he be so incapable, she wondered? But he was, incapable of anything other than musical pursuits. She could see the redness coming back to the skin of his hands and took one of his in hers, remembering the twisted, crabbed fingers when she first found him here.

"I'm sorry," she said, "it's all my fault and I should never have left you alone with him."

"Flesh and blood," he said.

"Cain and Abel," she said.

"More like Abraham and Isaac," he said.

"Don't know that one."

And he told her, about Abraham's contract with God to sacrifice his beloved son Isaac.

"An excellent idea," she said. "You must tell me what happened—"

"An angel intervened."

"Has he been sleeping here?" she asked.

"He comes and goes," William said. "Like a thief in the night."

"Again, I don't get the reference."

"'For you are fully aware that the day of the Lord shall come like a thief in the night.' And don't ask me how I remember that."

She told him that was enough of the Bible. She was afraid the next reference would be to the prodigal son, returned, and the killing of the fatted calf. This return, if that's what it was, was all her fault. And she was moving in.

"Is that wise?" he asked her.

"Maybe not for me," she said. "But for you. At the very least, it might keep him out."

She dabbed a length of gauze with antiseptic and wound it round his forehead. And she remembered his gauzed hands.

"Don't worry," she told him. "I'll sleep in the back room."

The one overlooking the orchard, the bed of nettles, the well. There was the lingering smell of Golden Virginia tobacco in the room. The odour of sweat and something she could only think of as caravan, from the crumpled sheets. She changed them, and did her best to sleep.

33

"Scottish," she said aloud.

It was like playing a game with a shadow of herself. When she slept this shadow slept, but she never knew where. She would check the empty rooms before William woke, and find her nose made the best detective. The hint of that scent that she could only call caravan, for want of a better word. She preferred for him to remain nameless, and pushed the thought of Alastair back to where the shadows seemed to come from. So he became a damp drying print of mud on the scullery floor. The twist of a cigarette butt in a candle-holder. A curled pressed shape amongst the uncut grasses, as if a man-sized hare had made its bed there. And when night came down there was nothing for it but to watch TV.

William liked *Line of Duty*. She hated it. She was surprised at the prosaic nature of his tastes in television and amused at how rapidly their evenings became centred round the question, what shall we watch tonight? So she watched, against all of her better instincts. She had always despised those contrived plot points and sudden reversals and revelations. Besides, she told him, she could never tolerate those British uniforms. The silly hats didn't go with sidearm and automatic weapons. Give me an American cop show any day, she was thinking, when the accent of the one from *Trainspotting* set something off in her.

"Scottish," she said again, and turned to William, on the couch beside her. How long would this last, she wondered? So comforting, somehow. The show that he loved, she hated. Out of such compromises, maybe, domesticity is formed.

"He's Scottish," she said again, and reached a hand out to touch his cheek.

"You mean she," he said. "And she is. More Glasgow than Edinburgh."

"I meant he. And he can't be. The letter came from Hull."

"What letter?"

"From the adoption register."

"They could have moved. The adoptive parents."

They could have. But she somehow knew they didn't.

"He hurt you," she said, and touched his cheek again, where the bruise hadn't yet faded. She should ask the well, she thought, madly, to herself.

"It was a temper tantrum."

"What son hits a father?"

"Many of them, I've heard."

"Maybe you've grown too close."

"The idea does take some getting used to."

"The idea?"

"A son," he said. "Fatherhood."

"So you've resigned yourself to it?"

"I'm not sure."

Good then, she thought. And she said it.

"What if he's not?"

"Not?"

"Your son. Mine. What if he's some kind of imposter?"

"That's preposterous."

"I know," she said. "But my boy grew up in Hull. That one didn't."

My boy, she had said. And a feeling overcame her, and suddenly she knew what had been missing.

"That would be a crime, surely," William said.

"Is there a name for it?"

"A crime without a name, maybe. Not on the statute books yet."

34

Spring was definitely on its way, she thought, watching the faded pink blossoms blow around the Church of Ireland graveyard. Two or three sad and bare cherry trees amongst the oppressive yews.

Her little nest in the back rectory bedroom had kept the interloper at bay, although she still heard rustlings from the orchard at night. She would wake suddenly, feeling a shadow had passed over her dreams, to find nothing there. Nothing but the smell of old tobacco drifting up from the staircase. So his very absence was becoming a kind of presence. But she didn't know where he slept. If he slept.

"You got used to him?" she asked William over breakfast. Two eggs, lightly poached by his unblemished hands.

"One can get used to anything."

"Do you miss him, then?"

"I am not sure he ever really left."

He paused, and wiped a bead of yellow egg from her lip.

"Dear."

And maybe it was that dear that did it. She made her way from the rectory down the small graveyard path to the back of her cottage. She saw her swimming things flapping from the line where she had left them, how many days ago now? And did she miss her little house? Not at all, she thought, unhooking her togs and the small orange towel that flapped there, drying in the April wind. She bundled them both in her hands and made her way through the small dry stone walls until they collapsed into sea grass and sand dunes. She felt like swimming again. She knew, somehow, that eyes would be on her. But she wanted those eyes.

There had always been transients in those woods, she thought to herself. When she had asked around the town who owned the blue caravan she was met with shrugs. No-one knew, and nobody had noticed its current inhabitant. And maybe that blue caravan belonged to nobody in particular, just to whichever wandering soul happened to make their way there. She had considered a complaint to the guards in Bantry, but decided to suffer this confrontation first. There were certain details she had to know.

She undressed in a small recess amongst the dunes. I'll swim, she thought to herself, the way I did on Dollymount Strand with Linda Grey and Jessie McCormack when we treasured every step into the water and knew we were magnets for prying eyes.

She walked through the grasses then, onto the dry sand which became the damp sand, which became the small sculpted shells of sand with spoons of water between them. Then the tide itself, lapping lazily over her ankles, her calves, the sting of cold around her waist, and her head, which she let sink beneath it, raising one arm and then the other, swimming out, until she had to arch her neck and take a breath. She could see the curved headlands far off, and the mounds of rock whose names she never remembered and which felt like sirens, luring some shore-bound creature to a certain doom in the water. That's what I'll call them from now on, she was thinking, Siren's Rock, when she saw the same outline, pacing from the dark pencils of the trees along the shore.

Well played, siren, she thought, although he could have already been tracking me from the garden to the dunes. Dragging that thing behind him, was it a sack or a sleeping bag? She turned away, took a few more strokes out towards the ocean, and then turned back, readying herself for the inevitable reckoning.

"Hey you," he said, when she made her way, dripping, from the water.

"Hey yourself," she said.

It could have been the beginnings of a flirtation from a movie, probably French, the tale of a younger man and an older woman, shock horror, could she or would she. A melody came into her head and wouldn't leave. "Stranger on the Shore". She remembered a drunk clarinettist on the cruise ship, and her own piano accompaniment. Then the melody stuck in her brain, as she made her way past him, the warble of the clarinet's lower notes. She reached the grasses of the lower dunes and found her things nestling amongst them. And she was dressing, struggling with her bra, when he appeared on the dune above her.

"We have to talk," she said.

She was almost proud of her powers of enticement. She had drawn him out from his lair in the woods, like a mermaid to a sailor or like a spider to a fly. She managed the clasp of the bra and bent down to the sand, towelling her hair. She would have waggled her behind, had the movie been French.

"I would say so," he replied.

"How has it been," she asked, "confronting your demons?"

"A kind of relief," he said.

"Aha. What the therapist told you to expect?"

"The therapist told me to expect nothing."

She had turned her back to him to deal with the clothing issue, and he had to admit that, from above, his vantage point, her butt looked very serviceable. But that, he realized, could be no part of their conversation. A son can't get a stauner for his mother.

"What if I told you that I suspect there was no therapist?"

"Oh but there was."

And there had been. He had to struggle to find a name. Mrs Hirst.

"Mrs Hirst."

"Could I contact the same Mrs Hirst then, and get her account of your conversations?"

"You could. If I could remember her number."

"The therapeutic dialogue between Alastair J Hitchens and Mrs Hirst? By the way, what does the J stand for?"

She could see him struggling. Maybe his imagination was failing him.

"Jimmy."

"And the name of the rehab place?"

"Stanley's Well."

"In Hull?"

"Hull on the Humber."

"But your accent. You see I was watching *Call of Duty*. Which is more William's thing than mine. I've always hated English cop shows."

She finished with the towel, straightened herself and allowed her hair to hang backwards.

"But that detective. The one from *Trainspotting*. She has your accent. And my boy—"

She felt the same emptying of her heart at that word.

"—he was never Scottish."

Keep your head clear, Tara, she thought.

"My boy's from Hull."

She could hear the wind blowing through the dunes. And his feet above her, shifting on the sand. She almost felt sorry for him.

"It's the little things. In every lie. You have to watch the little things."

"He could have travelled."

"He could indeed," she said.

"Got work on the fishing boats, round the isles."

"That too," she said.

She could see small avalanches of sand, tumbling down towards her, from his dingy grey trainers.

"Like I did," he said.

"But the thing is, you're not him," she said.

"Thing is, I could have been."

"You'd better come clean. Tell me about him."

And she dropped the towel as he descended the sandy hillock towards her. She sat down, planked her bum amongst the rustling grasses and patted the sand beside her, inviting him to do the same.

So he sat. And he told her.

She could picture the scene. Two needles in two bodies in a caravan in winter. One of them dead. The word caravan filled her with the same unease his dirty trainers did. Yes, she had given a child up for adoption, and yes, she had agreed for her contact details to be shared. She knew something of him would turn up one day. But not this malignant substitute.

That strange feeling of being told what you suspected already. The odd revulsion his bodily habits caused in her, the scent of his clothes, not quite unwashed, but somehow too forthright and too decidedly male. His habit of chomping those crisp packets with his mouth still open. The forced Scottish burr. Aye lass. An old mucker of mine.

The caravan in a place called Cleethorpes. She could readily imagine it. A drab line of summer homes, buffeted by the winter winds. Why did British seaside towns always seem so forlorn? She remembered walking along the Brighton promenade, the sound of the breakers sucking back the enormous pebbles. As far as Hove some mornings, and further, to the fields beyond, full of those rectangular caravans, mobile homes, whatever they were called. A youth discovered on an unwashed bed, a needle hanging from his arm.

"And who are you?"

"Does it matter?"

"It could matter a lot."

"You know the way it is these days. Girls can be boys and boys can be girls. Identity..."

He had to work hard to remember.

"... is a shifting thing."

"Where did you read that?"

"Some waiting room. Some rehab place. Maybe Alastair read it too—"

"Why did you claim to be him?"

"Never claimed to be."

"But you allowed us to think you were."

"Aha. Won't get me on that. Can't help what others think. You were waiting, he said, for a ghost to turn up. I turned up. Filled all of the requisite requirements."

"So why did you let us think that?"

"I was collecting. A debt. On his behalf."

"I could tell the police."

"Tell them what? That you thought I was him? The one you abandoned?"

"Stay away from us."

"Stay away from you?" he asked. "That would be hard."

And he rubbed his finger off her hairline. She had to strike the hand away.

"But I could manage it."

"And him," she said.

"Can't stay away from him."

"Why not?"

"There's a job to be finished. A grotto round the well. A financial arrangement."

"Consider yourself fired."

"Have to hear that from him."

35

It resolved itself by the well, as most things did. Several nights later, she was lying in the back bedroom, listening to the night-time symphony coming from across the way, wondering how William managed to sleep with the cacophony he made, when she heard another sound outside.

A kind of scraping clash, as if a set of cymbals was made of shale or granite.

She looked out and saw a figure backing out of the potting shed.

So that was where he laid his head, she thought, and she felt almost sorry for him. What had happened to the caravan?

She pulled her clothes on, moving downstairs, and could see him through the kitchen window, moving through the orchard, in whatever light the moon with its scudding clouds afforded. He was dragging something through the tangled grasses.

"Shells," he said, when she came out of the kitchen door.

"Shells?" she asked.

"For the grotto. Been collecting them."

"You should stop then," she said. "You don't belong here."

He gave an odd smile, and dumped whatever he was carrying in a bed of nettles. He sat down cross-legged by the well and she was amazed once more at his agility, the way he managed it in one supple movement of those long legs. He took a rolled cigarette from behind his ear, lit it and inhaled.

"Maybe I do."

"I want you to leave now—"

"The thing is," he said, "I've never felt so much at home."

"I could call the guards—"

"Guards," he said. "Is that what they call the polis here?"

And as she pulled her phone from her pocket, he rose again, in one of those amazingly supple movements. No need for a supporting hand, two knees unbent and he was looming above her, one long arm reaching for her phone, so she had to arch her own hand back.

So then, the push.

36

The call had been abrupt, the information minimal, there were many caravan parks in Cleethorpes, in fact the seafront seemed like one endless caravan park, and by the time they found the relevant one, his lips, his eyelids, even the cuticles of his fingernails had turned blue.

There was the hint of a pulse, though, so they unhooked the gurney by the caravan steps and lifted the body gently onto it, and he looked almost peaceful on the hospital drive.

They swabbed the lesions on his inner elbow and removed the dangling needle, inserting it into a small plastic bag for future reference.

The waves pounded the strand and their tendrils of white foam seemed to be intent on dragging down the pier. The winds buffeted the ambulance as it wailed its way along the promenade and made CPR treatment on the gurney inside difficult, but not impossible.

At the Diana, Princess of Wales Hospital in Grimsby he was brought to the intensive care unit, injected with naloxone, then attached to a ventilator. A swab from the used needle showed traces of fentanyl, heroin and levamisole, a drug for worm infection that can slow the flow of blood to the brain. His triage team formed a diagnosis of cerebral hypoxia and his blood pressure was stabilized, although prolonged seizures made the stabilization of his heartbeat a problem and a process of therapeutic hypothermia was suggested, which lasted more than twenty hours. When the obvious and prolonged brain swelling showed no reduction, his clothing was searched for any evidence of next of kin. When none was found, a tag was attached to his inert wrist, reading: Male, Unknown.

A coma was induced with phenobarbital to shut down brain function in its entirety.

37

And now, as she watched this other fall, she was struck by several things.

The first was, how easy it was. He was twice her height, had that muscle-bound thing she hated in what young men had lately become. The ones she saw on *Big Brother* and *Love Island*, who looked like they had come from a Hitler Youth graphic or a Charles Atlas brochure on bodybuilding. His muscular chest, underneath the soiled T-shirt, simply retreated under the impact of her open palm. The arms waved a bit, tried to grab at the mossy stone, unsuccessfully, since the next thing she saw were his grey trainers, careening backwards, hitting against the ellipse of ancient stone on the side furthest from her.

The second was that ridiculous lip of shell-pressed cement he called the grotto. Without it, he might have stabilized himself. With it, his left foot took to the air and propelled him backwards.

The third thing was the sound. There was an inward suck of breath, from him and not from her. No cry of protest or alarm, just that rather stunned inhale. A sough, she thought. That was the word for it, a sough, as he descended into the darkness of whatever the water below held for him.

Then there was the well itself. Whether she had invented the legend or not, the legend she had arrived at was all wrong. It was nothing to do with saints or reformed sinners, nothing to do with crosses and old rosary beads, nothing at all to do with the dim memory of her Catholic girlhood. It was something much more ancient. To do with the penetrating light of the winter solstice, the way the earth consumed its bounty and became bountiful again. With sacrificial things. There was a time to live and a time to die and this moment was without doubt his to die in. Because before she heard the splash from down below, she knew he was dead already.

It began to rain. Rain, of course, was a constant on that windy coastline, but the intensity of this rain surprised her. None of that windy, in your face stuff. This was a solid, vertical downpour. As she walked back through the muddy earth around the crab apple trees, she wondered at how it obliterated every footfall of hers. She made it to the uncut, sodden grass and wondered what she had just done. She had another, even more irrational urge than the urge to push that muscled chest of his.

To dance, in the falling rain across the uncut grass that could someday become winter hay. She arched her head back, felt the muscles of her neck crack and wondered had she hurt herself. She drew one foot across the uncut grass and traced a semi-circle. This is ridiculous, she thought, I can't be dancing in the rain. But it seems I am. I can't have killed that interloper. But it seems I did. The downpour began to lessen then, turn into something more familiar, like a soft mist. The clouds resumed their intermittent passage across the pale moon. And again, that strange sense that someone was looking at her. But he can't be, she thought. The interloper, the great pretender is gone. Then she saw movement, by the little copse of trees. A rabbit, she thought. Then she saw three heads, staring straight at her, wet ears pointed and erect.

Not one, but three hares.

38

She told him. She crept into his room without knocking, lay on top of the covers and told him. He was half awake, when she first got the words out.

"I killed him."

And he was fully awake now.

"You've what?"

It was interesting, she thought, that he used the past participle. She would have blurted out – you what?

"Killed him," she said. "Pushed him. He fell backwards down the well. I couldn't take it any more."

"Take what?"

"The whole thing. The fish. The seashells. The pretence. The conversation."

"About what?"

"You know what. We had a son he left for dead. He pretended. You fell for it."

"And you didn't?"

"I tried. I did my best. But do you know what it was in the end? That smell. Of caravan and fish. How could you hate your own flesh and blood? Unless they weren't. Your own flesh and blood."

"You're imagining this."

"Am I? He was by the well. Spouting off, in that accent of

his. I pulled my phone to call the guards and he tried to grab it. I pushed him. One tap. It was, given the circumstances, his size and mine, kind of easy."

"Oh T—"

And that surprised her. She had expected condemnation. Blame. Maybe even a police cell.

"My name is Tara."

"I know that."

"Say it then."

And how odd this all was, she thought. That he would smile at just that point.

"I prefer T."

"Given the absence of the L word?"

"Maybe. Come here."

But she couldn't. Pull aside the covers and curl up beside him. She left that gesture up to him. So he pulled them aside and wrapped his arms around her.

"It's all been too much for you."

"What about you? That bruise—"

"I don't know. Maybe I let him too close. I was enjoying the fantasy."

"You could tolerate him?"

"Not really. Only the thought."

"But I've killed him, William. Not just the thought of him."

"You'd better show me. Before—"

"Before what? The police and all that?"

"One thing at a time, T."

And he kissed her.

"Darling. Poor you."

★

And maybe it was that, she thought, as she made her way through the kitchen, took the flashlight and guided their way across the weeds. Maybe that's what had caught her, all of those years ago. That capability he had for surprise. It had been there, in his version of the Hayden. What started as a dutiful, perfect rendition of the score, without any apparent change, became a torrent of emotion. She hadn't noticed it happening, yet was sitting in the Wigmore Hall, alone amongst that splendid crowd, and found tears running down her cheeks. Everything was the same, his posture, the gently creaking piano stool, dividing the dress-suit tails, the notes were exactly as the score on her lap, and yet everything was different. The solicitude that had calmed the rush of blood through her murderer's veins had gone by now. He clung to her cardigan in the darkness, like a child that needed guidance. She led his slippers through the weeds with the pool of light, which eventually reached the scene of her crime. The imprint of his trainers was still etched in the mud, despite the rain, beside the smaller imprints of her sandals.

"We'll have to get rid of those."

Was he already taking control? Whether it would work or not, it was a relief to allow him.

"If anyone questions you," he said, "you didn't do it. I did."

"You can't be serious."

"I am. Don't test me on this. And there's only one way never to test me. Make sure that nobody asks questions."

"You didn't do it. I did."

"Show me. What you didn't do."

He took the lamp from her hand and began stamping the half-caked mud, obliterating the dead one's footprints with his own.

"No-one would believe you anyway. He was my size. Twice yours."

"I pushed him, William. From here."

"Show me how."

He stood in the other's place. And her hand shot out again, almost made the same thump on the curled hair of his chest. His hand caught hers by the wrist, stopping it before impact.

"And he fell?"

"Backwards. Down there."

He could feel the lip of the well against his heels. He gripped her wrist and was surprised by its strength. He could feel the immensity of her anger and realized with something like shame that he almost admired her for the capability.

He turned his attention to the lamp.

"Give it here, T."

Again, the same abbreviation. And she realized that, whatever happened, there would always be this between them. She handed him the lamp, saw him turn to the well, and bend from his knees to peer down.

The pool of light made a circle on the upper edges inside, the old stone glistening with the green moss. The circle became an ellipse, as he angled the lamp downwards. An elongated sausage of yellow light that sparkled occasionally with the moss-mildew and eventually illuminated a shifting patch of water, far, far below.

"There's nothing there."

She gripped the lip of the well and leaned over.

"There has to be."

"Look for yourself."

He handed her the torch. And the light played with the distant, seemingly conical source of it all. She expected to see a body, jammed against the ancient brick or bobbing at a broken angle in the water. But there was nothing. Just water, gently lapping in the yellow light.

"My god."

"Maybe you imagined it."

"You know I didn't. You stamped out his footprints. Yourself."

"You're right. I did. It's like they never existed."

"He can't have just—"

"Vanished? Let's check again."

He took the curl of old rope attached to the bucket, untied the bucket and wrapped the pieces of untangled, wayward string around the hook of the lamp. He lowered the lamp then, gently, into the well.

"It's like a probe," he said. "I had one during that operation."

"Which operation?"

"Kidney stones. But I didn't know you then."

"You did, you know."

"Alright, miss pedantic. I didn't know that I knew you."

And the lamp probed downwards, as he allowed the rope to crawl through his fingers. It crept down to where the moss began. And she realized to her surprise that the moss did begin. It traced a semi-circular green thread, below which the old brick was wet, but bare. And below that again, the distant orb of shifting water.

"You can see. There's nothing there."

She took a picture on her phone. It would probably be useless, but maybe she could enlarge it. To confirm what her eyes already told her. There was nothing there.

"I didn't imagine it."

"Maybe we imagined him."

She stopped. And the rain began again. As if some god had turned on a tap, from somewhere above.

"We imagined a son?"

"And all of the other unfinished business."

She watched the rain falling on his face, came to him, took his arm and drew him towards the scullery door.

"Maybe I can explain it."

She went back to his room that night. She told him, as he drifted into that half-awake, stentorian sleep of his, of the cries of seagulls, her trek over the fields, the blowhole by the cliff face and the booming ocean. Some kind of underground river, she said.

She woke the next morning, around dawn, and left him to that tortured breathing. The rain had stopped, but every patch of earth was sodden with it. She walked the same trek through the wet fields, and reached the fissure, with two beaches, one to the left and one to the right. There was the carcass of a sheep, almost a skeleton, caught between two rocks, and far below it, an explosion of white foam. Not quite white, but with that brown peaty tinge of a mountain river. It had been dry for months and now had more than enough sustenance. She imagined the broken corpse, stuck somewhere in the underworld beneath her.

They scoured the garden for evidence of him and burnt whatever they could find in a brazier. Down the well with the ashes was his suggestion, but it felt obscene to her, somehow sullied her image of the waters down below. Which was absurd, he pointed out to her, who had sent the body these ashes belonged to tumbling down already. And she knew it was absurd but she also knew he shared her sense of reservation. The first was instinctive, involuntary, almost accidental. Sullying the well with what they found of him would have been a polluting act. So they traced their way around the rectory, scattering the ashes as they went like two latter-day Johnny Appleseeds. The wind took most of it. And when his bucket was as empty as hers, he lifted his free hand in a high-five gesture. She met it with hers, then allowed her hand to explore the texture of the skin of his palms, those spaces between his long fingers.

39

Daisy tolerated the blue hospital scrubs, the plastic gloves, even the constant irritation of the face mask, as an occupational hazard. She had applied for the job that nobody wanted, hospital cleaner, paid 14.50 an hour and in the full flush of the covid thing had found herself celebrated, locally and nationally, as an essential worker. She was touched by the applause that often greeted her visitations to whatever old folks homes needed her services that week and, when given the promotion to cleaning duties in Diana, Princess of Wales Hospital, Grimsby, welcomed the opportunity to be more essential in the general essentialness of things. She enjoyed a smoke, amongst the stinking refuse bins out back, and it was in the course of one of these that she was informed by an acquaintance of hers that if she could bear the full PPE equipment and cleaning duties on the upper floors, the pay was almost double.

She was familiar with the A&E, the various canteens on the ground and first floors and the toilets that marked each corridor with health procedures and covid warning signs, male and female icons and one that was meant to indicate a newborn baby needing a new nappy. But her barely breathable PPE outfit and the lanyard round her neck that identified her as essential staff now allowed her access into the upper reaches of the building. She felt she was entering some rarefied zone on the fifth floor, marked only by the beeping of heart regulators and defibrillators and the kind of soft zombified music that one encountered in spas and massage parlours. And not for the first time, she wondered who chose this stuff. Was there a Spotify option for the blissed-out, the occasionally mindful, the recently massaged or those who were prolonging their final exit from this state of things? Everything was hushed up here, including the soft shuffle of her sandals, in the microporous fabric that now covered them. Each room was like a sarcophagus, with a barely moving figure on an orthopaedic bed, surrounded by white shrouded triage teams, and it was in one of these, while bending to remove yet another plastic bag from yet another rubbish bin, that she recognized a profile she had last seen in the Fleece Inn, on the Lock Road in Grimsby.

The doctor attending took no more notice of her than he did of the gently beeping machines and the thing like a mechanical paddle that rose and fell like a branch blown in a soft wind, with almost the same sound. So she left, without any of the details attached to the chart clipped to the foot of his orthopaedic bed.

There had been two of them, she remembered, and she fancied not this one, but the friend. The friend that spoke with a Scottish accent, and bought her too many drinks, but it was this one that had managed her exit, placed her in a taxi and given her his phone number, to call when she got home safely.

She made her way down in the lift, plastic bags clutched in each gloved hand, dumped them in the appropriate bin and made her way outside for another cigarette and a scroll through her text messages. Why did she never go for the gentler ones, she wondered, and found the text, back home now thx, and the number, and a name.

Alastair.

40

"Gone," William said, realizing what her fingers were searching for.

"So it seems," she said.

She allowed her hand to drop and his came with it. So they walked through the small copse of crab apple trees hand in hand. An odd togetherness seemed to be nudging its way around them, inside them, between them. They were bound together by a secret. Hardly a crime as yet, and if it was to be so judged, the crime was hers. But the secret they had to keep could become its own transgression, and would it, she wondered, as they reached the kitchen door again, become a chain that would bind them both?

Better not thought about, she shivered, as she closed the kitchen door behind her and realized there was something else, hemming her in towards it.

Him. His body. His arms around her cheeks now, from behind, exploring the curve of her neck, the bone below the first button of her cardigan, her breasts beneath.

He wanted her, and didn't for once need to know why. She took his hands and led them downwards, and soon it would have to be on the kitchen floor, unless they repaired to more appropriate places.

"Let me," he said, and lifted her, turning her towards him and she wrapped her legs around his waist, arching her head back against the kitchen windows.

"This is ridiculous," he said, and swung her around, one arm beneath her neck and the other beneath the crook of her legs, like an overgrown child.

"Let me carry you."

"I thought you couldn't."

"These are extreme circumstances. Let me try."

She said nothing, and with some difficulty he did carry her, across the flagstones, across the wooden boards the piano sat on, up the stairs and into his bedroom.

"Why?" she asked afterwards, in the tangle of his bedsheets.

"I don't rightly know," he said, kneading the recess of bone just above her hairline.

But he did, and so did she. They were wrapped in their own particular secret now, two criminals together.

"I'd better clean up," she said.

"No need," he said.

"There is," she said. "I still have a job to do."

She cleaned herself first, then noticed something stuck in the gap between two mirrors. The butt of a rolled-up cigarette, jammed in there. So she applied herself to the house, to eliminate all trace of the dead one.

It was like a forensic trawl from one of her favourite police shows. *CSI: Miami, Law & Order.* She even wore disposable plastic gloves. And it was extraordinary to scour out whatever residue he had left. A piece of itinerant hair in a plughole. More rolled-up butts, jammed into floorboards, the gaps beneath the window sills. Nail clippings on toilet floors. A jar of kefir in the fridge, beside the bag of bean sprouts, the rancid plastic packet of soy bean curd. They could have been anybody's, of course. But she knew they had been his.

Something else he had left behind him, which she couldn't clean with her Jeyes fluid and her plastic gloves. That strange, guilty thrill of his absence. It was like a dark vacuum, filling out the space between her and the pianist inside.

Then she pulled open the freezer. There was a supermarket bag, covered in hoar frost. She peeled it open to see a frozen mass of grey, almost Neanderthal flesh. And she knew where it had come from, without having to ask.

She remembered that morning on the strand, the John Dory jerked from the nightline hook, and she had a shiver of panic, wondering had they been overlooked. A John Dory, for you. You and your man-friend.

"William," she called.

The playing stopped. A procession of footsteps towards the kitchen door and there he was.

"T?"

"Fish," she said.

"Ah yes," he said. "They were a kind of gift."

She could imagine the scene. The dead things proffered, the four fish eyes dripping onto the stone floor, all gazing in the same direction. Would those cold, inert frozen lumps inside the hoar-frosted plastic connect them to him? The thought of a gift of fish seemed like a threat, straight out of some ancient legend.

"What do we do with them?"

"Throw them away?"

"But where?"

"On the what's it called—"

"The compost heap?"

She imagined them rotting, amongst the rotting vegetables, inviting a malignant horde of rats. She could almost see the brown scurrying shapes amongst the crab apple trees. These fish had a story to tell, she somehow knew, that would only spread as their iced flesh melted.

"I don't know about fish," she said. "Being Irish, fish on Fridays. Never liked them."

He came behind her, looking over her shoulder at the hoar-frosted SuperValu bag.

"Turbot," he said.

"Turbot?"

"Be a crime to throw them away."

"A crime?"

"They were frozen the day he caught them. And believe me, my dear…"

He moved around her and took the frozen lumps from the plastic bag.

"… you have never tasted fish until you've tasted turbot."

He placed the frozen things on the runner of the sink, washed his hands meticulously and played Brahms for the afternoon as the turbot melted. She returned to the kitchen intermittently, fascinated by the way those lumps of ice and hoar frost slowly dissolved into something resembling ocean creatures. The brown skin, the dead semi-circle of spiked fin, the dead accusing eyes, glistening with moisture. He turned the oven up to 180 and she watched him scour a baking tray, gut and scale the fish and flavour it with salt and pepper.

"You can cook?" she asked, dumbly.

"Like any lifelong bachelor," he said, and exposed the flesh beneath the skin with four deft slices of a knife. He diced some garlic then, sliced a lemon, drizzled the brown, slashed skin with olive oil and placed the lot inside the burning oven.

"Twenty minutes," he said, and uncorked a bottle of white wine from the fridge.

"We need potatoes," she said.

"Of course," he said, and she saw the small pot, already bubbling on the ring. Another one beside it.

"And broccoli," he said. "Let me warm some plates."

He had it in spades, she began to realize, as she watched him set the table, that thing she was always missing, the nurturing instinct. It flowed like an exhausted breath from him, as if it was a talent he had never been given the opportunity to exercise. Two gloved hands, raising the fish from the blazing oven, like an alchemist. One dead thing had turned into something else, had been given a different life. There was no trace left of the one who had delivered it, no nauseous stench of him, or the foreshore, just this delicious flesh to be consumed, the almost burnt lemon curling above it, the cold white wine to wash it down.

"I never knew fish could be so glorious."

"Thank him for that, at least."

So they both ate, consigning him to memory. Two skeletons of bone, on two blue willow plates.

41

Daisy waited, after her cigarette break the next morning, until his room was empty before beginning cleaning duties. She closed the door behind her and half walked, half shuffled in the way the fabric of the PPE soles necessitated, towards the clipboard at the foot of his bed. The diagnostic details made no sense to her but what did was the tag around his immobile wrist.

Male. Unknown.

What about his phone, she wondered? She scrolled down her own phone again until she found her message, back home now thx. The name Alastair and the number. She dialled and half expected to hear the answering ring come from the pocket of his blue scrubs, but no. There was just the barely perceptible rise and fall of his chest, as if in answer to the paddles of the ventilator above him. And a computerised voicemail.

So she sat. She placed her fingers beneath his wrist and raised it, ever so gently. She could feel the warmth there, and the pulse. She could read the wrist tag, Male. Unknown.

She wondered should she take the biro from the clipboard and add the name Alastair to the tag, when she heard the door opening behind her and a woman walked in, barely younger than herself but with a poise and a sense of self-possession she knew she would never muster, and the woman asked, although not entirely unkindly, what she was doing there.

"Cleaning," Daisy answered, and got slowly to her feet. The figure on the bed deserved no sudden movements.

"The refuse bin is over there," the doctor indicated and Daisy dutifully made her way towards it. But halfway across the room she stopped.

"May I ask," she began, as if politeness would make sense of the question, "has he never been identified?"

"You may," said the doctor in an accent that Daisy now recognized as Irish, "but why?"

"Just curious, maybe."

"The police took a fingerprint swab, we've sent flyers round the area, but the answer is no. There has been no identification. No next of kin."

"The area?" Daisy asked. "What area?"

"The area in which he was found. A caravan in Cleethorpes, I believe. An overdose. And if you'll now excuse me—"

Daisy read Flanagan on the doctor's lanyard. And bent to the refuse bin, gripped the clear plastic bin bag in her plastic-gloved hand.

She wondered, smoking again around the refuse bins, what the police had to do with it. She scrolled through her phone again and saw the same number and the name, Alastair.

Maybe this Alastair wanted anonymity. Maybe the police wanted him. Maybe it was best to forget about that gently, barely breathing profile, but she rang the number again, and heard the voice again, pretending it wasn't a computer. When the same acquaintance pushed his way through the refuse bins and began to roll himself one, she asked him was it possible to trace a full name from a mobile number?

"Easy," he said. "Like everything these days. There's an app. FindMyMobile.com."

So she used it, as she finished her cigarette. Typed in the number, and as she squashed the butt of her cigarette on the bin five minutes later, her phone pinged.

On her screen was a name. Alastair Hitchens.

42

It was odd, to be brought together by a crime. Every fairy tale she'd been told, everything she'd read pointed in the opposite direction. This my hand would rather the multitudinous seas incarnadine turning the green one red. The ghost in *Hamlet*. The police shadow on the front door window in any number of cop shows. A union like theirs should have descended into mutual hatred, recrimanation, or at the very least, guilt.

But no. They walked the stretch of beach together and saw the two rusting nightline rods still pinioned into the sand. A thread of fishing gut still clung to one of them with a twisted hook. She advised William to leave them where they were. She walked alone through the scraggy forest one morning and saw the blue caravan inhabited again, two grubby children running around the half-open door. A woman was raising clouds of dust from the interior, so she imagined it had been reclaimed by the owners, or claimed by subsequent squatters.

So they had a bubble of secrecy they had to maintain which was theirs alone. He continued calling her T, as if her full name, Tara, was too much of a formality. She thought of calling him W, or Dubya, in the way of that grinning ex-president, but it had too many syllables, so she reduced it to Will.

Their secret was helped by the coming of summer. The main

street grew full to bursting with staycationers. The presence or absence of her ersatz Alastair could hardly have been noticed amongst the throngs on the beach, the pier, the bar tables. But what was noticed was that something had changed in her, in both of them, and if people remarked on it, or noticed, she gave them a valid reason.

That they were a couple now.

"Sure, it was obvious," Mary Culleton said, cutting a large parmesan with a cheese knife. "It's a small town. No hiding anything."

"What's there to hide?" Tara asked in reply, and for a moment felt a cold flurry of dread.

"I could see it in you. In him, whenever he came in. The years fell off him."

"So it's true?" asked Peter, on the wooden table outside of the pub.

"Must be," she said, "if you've heard."

"God bless you, Tara. You deserve better than yours truly."

"Now, Peter. Don't do yourself down."

"And what happened with the Scottish lad?"

She felt as if a stone had been dropped, into an endless depth.

"What Scottish lad?"

"Was asking about you. Then asking for work on the boats."

"He must have gotten it then. Or left for the summer."

"I'm happy for you – both—"

He leaned forward to plant a beery kiss on her cheek.

"Your secret's out, you know."

And once again that cold, subterranean shiver.

"What secret would that be, Peter?"

"That hole in the ground. I wouldn't dignify it with the term well. But others aren't as sceptical. Word spreads. Healing waters and all that bullshit."

"People talk about it?"

"They do. And I tell them—"

He drained his pint.

"—it's not the water. It's the moss."

The moss. Someone was spreading the word and she wondered was it Peter. Several mornings, after waking, she would notice figures shifting rapidly away through the dawn mists. She mentioned it to Will who mentioned it back to the same Peter, who proposed a protective covering over the mouth, in case an accident happened. Liability would be a nightmare, he said, and when Will relayed this to her, she agreed. Another accident might not have so felicitous an outcome.

Felicitous. It was his word, not hers. She liked to wake early, before the sun had banished the dawn mist, and one morning she opened the scullery door to see yet another ghost flitting towards the dry stone wall and the road beyond. And she noticed something fluttering, from the trellis, badly sagging now, around the well.

She walked towards it, feeling the morning dew around her bare feet. She found pieces of cloth, red, yellow, white, wound and tied between the gaps. Several notes pinned, a ten-euro one, several fives and an American ten-dollar bill.

Crime doesn't pay, she realized, but it does leave some dividends. And as her ersatz Alastair might have put it, had he lived, that moss could turn out a nice little earner. And after dinner that evening, she felt a sudden urge to dip her hands in it again. She left Will to his practice and opened the scullery door and was making her way through the overburdened orchard when she saw two figures, kneeling by the trellis, arms vanishing into the depths of the well.

Her well. She wondered where that strange sense of possession came from.

"Sorry."

A young woman, rising from her knees. Her hands full of wet moss.

"The guards could call that trespassing."

'We were just—"

A youth standing up now, beside her. Dreadlocked hair.

"—making a wish."

"For what?" she asked, and already knew how stupid she sounded.

"None of your business—" said the youth – more of a man, she saw now, an already lined face under the absurd dreadlocks – reaching two hands, from behind, around the young woman's stomach, pulling her back.

"Sorry again—"

What kind of wish? she wanted to ask. But they were already retreating, like ghosts in the orchard shadows.

The mossy stone seemed to glow, with a dull subterranean sheen, where the sun could never reach, as if a penumbra of plankton was coming from below. She walked to the well's edge and saw clumps of luminescent moss scattered on the grass around.

A wishing well. So a rumour had spread. And a wish, she had to admit, was in the end what a well suggested. Implied. Even demanded.

She surrendered then, as if resistance was futile.

She brought the crushed moss to her mouth and lips. Kissed it. She felt the water penetrating them, creating shivers of ice on her teeth, dripping over her chin, down the collar of her blouse. She wished with what a yoga instructor had once called her core, and it was a wish like a dark orgasm, for something unspoken, something from the past, something to be undone, some life to return. She dropped the fistful of moss then into the long cylinder of the well and when she didn't hear a splash, she thought her wish had vanished with it.

They really had to cover it in, she told him. She had come across two well-wishers. When he queried her term, she told him she couldn't find the word. Moss-gatherers? Supplicants, he suggested. Some kind of plate of mesh or metal that would prevent another fall. He agreed. Another dead supplicant could lead to an enquiry. He wasn't a supplicant, she told him. He was trying to face his demons, and maybe he had met them now.

She thought she should sleep alone that night. She would have cycled home, too long an absence from her parrot worried her, but the thought of the empty cottage worried her even more. She heated one of Mary's quiches for both of them, spooned out some coleslaw to give it the semblance of vegetable presence, and ate in silence beside him.

He finished and mentioned he was going to watch the penultimate episode of Line of Duty. If it wasn't for that show, she was about to tell him, we might still have that rancid stranger in our presence, then she stopped herself.

"I'll finish mine upstairs," she said.

Everything that came out of that mouth of hers seemed wrong. She could only thank her lucky saints that she hadn't mentioned her wish.

She entered the spare room and flurried the sheets on the

THE WELL OF SAINT NOBODY

hard wooden bed, set the blankets, opened the windows to freshen the air, crawled beneath the coverlet and tried to sleep. There was some lingering odour of roll-up tobacco which made her want to wrap herself in her nightgown, find an empty place on the armchair to watch *Line of Duty* with him. She thought of the Scottish tones of the female detective from *Trainspotting*, and took a pill instead.

She already knew what she would dream of, if a dream came, and she hoped it wouldn't. And when it came, it seemed familiar and inevitable, in its narrative, its dripping water, its dread.

She was in her own TV series and knew it, but somehow couldn't get out. Policemen in yellow hi-vis jackets, on motor and push bikes, in ambulances with streaks of yellow and flashing lights. She was being questioned by the well, where else, when the trellis began to tremble, the vines that had grown around it being pulled from below. Then one moss-covered hand gripping the edge of stone and gradually pulling itself upwards. Bloated of course, it had been inside there how long by now? Three months? So it raised its distended shape slowly, with immense effort. Scraping the gaseous stomach off the grotto of shells it had itself collected, and there seemed to be tendrils spilling over the belt, bits of weed she thought at first, until she realized they were portions of loosed intestine. There was a gash in the distended pouch of flesh, which confused her, even in the dream. She hadn't stabbed, she had pushed. Unless the skin had been ripped by some contact with an edge of ancient stone on its journey down. She couldn't move, of course, she had to suffer her own terror as if immobilized by some zombie tincture, watch the tread of the moss-covered squelching trainers over the grass, the flagstones of the kitchen and, lastly, over the boards of the bedroom floor as if drawn by its own odour, left by the rancid sleeping bag. Which was no longer there, she remembered thinking, so she might yet be safe, when she heard a rhythmic booming, which softened to a tapping, and she realized it was real and someone was knocking on the door.

Will. She knew. She thought. She hoped. She watched the door handle creak its way left, the door itself scrape open and there he was.

"You alright?" he asked.

"Not really," she admitted.

"Bad dream?"

"The worst."

"About?"

"You don't want to know."

"But I do. Come inside. Into the big four-poster. It's lonely without you."

"I shouldn't."

"I would like it if you did. Dear."

43

Daisy wondered did the dead dream. Did the comatose dream. She was aware that she often dreamed, sitting in the plastic chair, amongst the tangle of plastic tubing that facilitated something like breath. She dreamed of a wind, rippling over a vast ocean, the ripples it gave rise to only obscuring the vast life teaming beneath. There were curtains of darting silver, she knew, probably caused by the sprats and the shoals of mackerel that chased them. Hooks, dangling down from above and the loud thrum of a propeller, then the huge maw of a net, coming towards her, alive with the threshing shapes of the bigger fish and a horned one, twisting its way ahead of the netted apocalypse, bending in a deep rush towards freedom and the absolute darkness below. For some reason a mobile phone, tumbling down after it, and the phone was ringing, though she couldn't hear its dial tone underwater, could she, if she was truly underwater and she would wake again to the plastic sound of mechanized breath, the gently beeping heart monitor and soft pulsing lights of the hospital room. Alastair was his name, and her name was Daisy, and why she took comfort sitting here and dreaming she had no idea. Only that he had helped her to the taxi and texted to see had she made it home.

Did the dying need help on their way, she wondered. She

looked at his profile under the watery mask and imagined a paddle, breaking the surface of the same ocean. It was still now, and only her paddle created the ripples, the canoe was long enough to hold two of them, wherever they were going, but her paddling was unsteady and the soft underbelly of the canoe rocked or her spiked heel had pierced the vellum. Was it vellum, some kind of bark like old, old paper, and the water filled it from the underbelly below and the lip of the vessel from above dipped awkwardly and they were under again and sinking the way the phone had and the horned fish swam past them, deeper into the depths which she should have known all of the time was their destination.

Then the door would open and the night nurse would wonder what she was doing there and she would answer that she didn't know, but that if the situations were reversed, if she were the one under the plastic mask and he, Alastair Hitchens, was the one observing, she would somewhere within herself be glad of that fact.

44

Tara had been dreading it for some time now, but when it eventually happened, it was still unexpected. It was not the shadow of a peaked American hat or curved British helmet against the front door window. No, she already knew, her very own crime series would be decidedly Irish. She was observing the blob of a yellow hi-vis jacket in the window by the piano, bubble engorged, making its way down through the procession of distorted umbrellas that she knew were the elm and poplars of the avenue. She thought of calling Will then decided not to and waited as the shape passed out of sight behind the frame of the warping glass, waited some more, then when she heard nothing, hoped she had imagined it. She realized what a vain hope that was when she was almost lifted from her seat by the shrill sound of the buzzer she had forgotten she had installed. Feck, that's loud, she thought, and heard Will's footsteps on the upper landing.

"It's OK," she called out, "I've got it" – as if it was a delivered letter or a message when she knew there would be none. So she opened the door and saw the blushing face of a lad far too young to be a policeman, but she knew he had to be one, by reason of the blue uniform beneath the hi-vis yellow, the helmet he was pulling from his sweating ginger curls.

"I'm sorry, ma'am, it's just a routine enquiry," he began, and then paused, as if waiting for an invitation.

"I'm sure they're always routine," she said, realizing she had expected this, and almost, in a strange way, welcomed it. The suspended, anticipated question would be answered, at last. There are to be no unpunished crimes. She stepped aside, an unspoken invitation to the young guard's unspoken request. Young guard, she thought. How old does that make me? Not quite old enough to be his mother, but neither young enough to be anything else to him. Maiden aunt, perhaps.

"We called at your residence. No reply. And I was told you work here—"

"I do."

"It's about," he began, "the blue caravan in the Graun Wood."

So that's what it's called, she thought to herself.

"The Graun Wood?" she asked, and hoped he didn't notice that she was playing for time.

"Not really a wood. A straggle of ash and holly trees, behind the pier, above the beach."

"Of course," she lied. "Only I didn't know there was a caravan park there—"

"Nothing like a park. One caravan, hard to see it from the beach. The thing is the owners have returned, come for the summer and noticed there's been a break-in. They found a pouch there, with some—" and he coughed here, the cough disguising itself in a grin, "illegal substances—"

"Drugs?" she asked and tried to raise an eyebrow. She must learn to enjoy this, she thought, her very own episode of *True Detective*. It could go on for months. She would have to perfect her part.

"Yes," he said, "but let's not worry about that. Inside the pouch they found something else. A credit card."

He took it out now, from his blue-buttoned top pocket. In a small plastic baggie, just as in her favourite episodes, and inside an AIB card, on which she could already make out her name.

"Mine. My god—"

And she wondered when he could have filched it. That encounter by the dunes, when she turned away, unhooking her bra? If so, she felt some admiration for his dexterity.

"—that's where it went—"

"Aha. That makes sense. You had mislaid it?"

"What? You think I was buying drugs from—"

"There was some kind of vagrant. Living there. Gone now."

"And to think of it, I did have a break-in."

"Here?"

"No, in my place. My cottage—"

It was true. She had. And she realized how necessary truth was to an extended deceit.

"I didn't report it because I didn't find anything missing. Just a few beers from the fridge – and—"

She reached out to touch the card. And to her sweet relief, he pressed it into her hand.

"—some private things—"

"You didn't miss it?"

"The card? No. But thank god, officer – it must have never been used."

"Didn't report the break-in?"

"It was hardly a break-in. A few muddy prints round the fridge. Some what are they called. Heinekens. A few euro notes missing. But if I'd known about the card, of course I would have. The bank had just sent it. Did I sign it? I can't remember—"

"This card isn't signed."

He turned it in her hand.

243

"Oh. I must have left it in the drawer of the kitchen table. He must have used the key, under the pot by the kitchen door. So where would he be? This interloper—"

"You know these crusties," the guard said. "They come and go."

"And they have their caravan back?"

"The Dublin lot? Yes. Here for the summer. No harm done. So—"

And his nail rubbed the surface of the card, made a scraping sound over the embossed numbers.

"No drawdowns? It was never used?"

"Let me check with the bank. But they would have told me, surely—"

"They would surely. So—"

And he backed towards the door. Set the cap back on his head. Touched the peak. And she was in an episode of *Line of Duty* now, nothing American about it.

"We can forget about him—"

"Him? Could it not have been a woman?"

"There were muddy prints all over the caravan floor. If a woman wears size eleven Adidas—"

"Adidas?" she asked, and for the first time she felt a shiver.

"Or Asics. Trainers anyway. If he turns up, and you want to press charges, come to the Schull station. Let me know."

"I will," she said. "Oh, I will."

Will appeared at the top of the stairs, as the sound of the front door echoed.

"Trouble?"

"I don't know."

Her hands were shaking, which she found strange. Is that the way panic works, she wondered? Calm when the terror presents itself, then the trembling aftermath.

"If you are questioned further, you will blame me."

"Why would I be questioned?"

"Why would a guard cycle all this way?"

"They found my credit card. In his tobacco pouch. He must have stolen it somehow."

"Where did they find it?"

"That ratty caravan. The owners had returned. Saw there had been a break-in."

Her hands were still shaking, as he descended. She offered them to his. He took them in his smooth long fingers and kneaded her palms into some sense of quiet. And she asked him then was that the way it happened. One small enquiry, one windblown detail, in this case a filched and forgotten credit card, leads to a full enquiry. She could already imagine the hazmat suits around the rusting metal plate that lay over the well's mouth, the crane trundled in, the police divers, wading through the nettles round the orchard like druidic witches with their strange webbed feet.

"What will we call it?" she whispered.

"Call what?"

"My own true detective series?"

"It was just an enquiry."

"You sure?"

45

And then she tried that wish again. That was what wells were for, surely, despite all of the other tasks she had invented for this one. The gardens were in their late summer confusion, and she made a mental note to hire Peter to tame them. The same Peter who had tractored in a rusting metal plate, to hide it from the well-wishers, the moss-gatherers. As she walked around the back, a rat scurried through the tangled grasses. The trellis had been half flattened by the recent storms and the metal plate held a small pond of rainwater, thick with fallen leaves. There were several gaps, though, since the well was round and the plate was square, through which she could finagle her still tiny hands. However much the rest of her had grown, these would never. She felt the moss below, clinging to the cut surface of the circular stone, still wet, of course. She couldn't imagine circumstances under which it would ever dry.

She brought the wet green mossy stuff, like a huge handful of shamrock or clover, to her cheek and realized she didn't know what to wish for. For a different outcome, was all she could think. A different outcome to whatever disasters they had both left in her wake.

She cycled home the next morning to feed the parrot. She felt absurd and foolish. But it was not a bad feeling. The innocence of childhood, all around. She placed a handful of moss in the parrot's bowl. She would have to let this house go soon, she told him, along with many other of her favourite things. But she would make sure he had a home. He replied with the familiar bar of Erik Satie.

There were consequences to this wish, as there probably are to all wishes. If what we want to happen is cause, what happens, regardless of its connection to the initial want, can all too easily become effect. Something happens, something is always happening, and the temptation to connect what happens to what one wished to happen can be irresistible. It is only human to read a horoscope, the moon is in your sign this weekend, don't be afraid to spoil yourself, and to take it as a map to the landscape of what will happen anyway. And the body that was washed ashore at Inch Strand a whole other county away, the long spit of strand she remembered from the movie *Ryan's Daughter* could well have had nothing to do with the one she sent tumbling down into the depths of the well whose saint she had so cavalierly invented. Suicides were common on the South Atlantic coastline, a distraught tourist one month, a depressed property developer the next, sometimes even a GAA hurling all-star. So the bloated body that was found with contusions on the forehead after a fall may not have been her ersatz Alastair, whose gaseous corpse could still be stuck in some underground recess somewhere between the well and the blow hole. There was a certain relief, all the same, in letting herself believe it was.

But there was no such doubt about the letter that fell through the breezy flap of her letterbox onto the home-sweet-home mat below, to the musical welcome of Eric the parrot. It was from the Adoption Contact Register in the UK. It requested details of her whereabouts, permission to share the same. She had a son, she learned, still alive, in Hull on the Humber, desiring to make contact.

46

She wondered about the paucity of her powers of invention as they drove out to Cork Airport. A wishing well. The simplest fairy tale, which could have saved her all that ludicrous body of fancy. The blemished beauty, the incipient saint, the goatherd, the healing waters. And she knew what that couple were wishing for, when she surprised them before the well was covered with that metal plate, to gather rust and damp foliage. A child.

She had learned more about him, the real and true and only Alastair, in the subsequent correspondence. He had overdosed, the overdose causing a stroke, and his companion had left him for dead, or for the paramedics to deal with. A long recovery, in and out of consciousness and more than a year in rehab, with several relapses. At the end of which he felt the need to deal, finally and conclusively, with his issues.

She hadn't slept the past week, worrying out what those issues were. She could barely imagine the Hitchens, who undertook parental duties for her. She knew their names, Christabel and Francis, but that conveyed nothing to her but a sense of quiet, ordinary goodness. She had declined all offers to meet, being ordinary herself, but not at all good. She knew nothing of Hull, but could picture a suburban house that Paul McCartney might well have sung about. Maybe he could meet them, in Penny

Lane in Liverpool or Mull of Kintyre or even in Kingston upon Hull. She could see an apple tree, for some odd reason, in the front garden. One of those Dagenham cars in the driveway. A comprehensive and an unhappy stint as a boarder, to improve their son's academic performance. He had been bullied in both, failed his A Levels and then begun the inevitable descent, busking round the city centre streets, a spell in Edinburgh in a homeless shelter, and a return, to the drab seaside town closer to home.

She waited now, by the half-circle of friends, family and random taxi drivers at the Arrivals. It was odd, watching the bodies come through and wondering which of them could be yours. Most of them too old, too shapeless. What was it about this country, she wondered, that bred such pear-shaped men? Then she saw him and felt what had been missing, for many, many years.

In a wheelchair, of course, pushed by a smiling attendant in green, an anorak or a combat jacket over thin shoulders, a thinner pair of jeans leading to a pair of trainers and a pair of mismatched socks. A long thin neck with a bobbing Adam's apple and a smile that seemed permanent, or the result of some kind of rictus from the stroke.

She had always wondered what this feeling would be. And now that his eyes met hers, one hand spun the wheel of the chair, the other waved goodbye to the attendant, she recognized it instantly, but had no name for it. Like a large infinite well, with wishes of its own.

"Alastair," she said, and for the first time the word felt correct on her lips. He pushed his way towards her, both hands on the wheels. She could already see that one hand worked better than the other. She could also see a thin balding patch at the crown of his unruly hair that gave her an instant, painful pang. He was young, and somehow old.

The advice from the Adoption Contact Register and later the rehab clinic was not to force any intimacy, never to help with the chair, never to anticipate what he was trying to say.

But it was so obvious, as the wheels spun towards her, the semi-permanent grin increased in its intensity and the one good hand reached towards her.

"M – m – o –"

She didn't finish it for him. Let him say it, as he took her smaller hand in his.

"Mother."

Will was waiting in the Jaguar, parked across from the taxi cabs. She pushed the wheelchair through the electronic glass doors, and wondered would her Alastair have the same immediate familiarity with the word Father. It didn't seem so, as she rolled the wheels over the zebra crossing towards the tall figure waiting there.

"This is Will," she said.

The word seemed less complicated than Father.

"Will," Alastair said as Will bent and lifted his inert son from the chair. He did it so easily, so fluidly that she was momentarily stunned again.

He never loses that capacity to amaze, she thought, as she folded the chair in the way she had been instructed by the rehab handbook. Any progress would be slow, she had been warned, but every incremental step would be both essential and momentous. Will placed him in the front seat as she locked the folded wheelchair in the capacious boot. And the drive back was mostly in silence, as they both tentatively explored their new son's capacity for speech.

★

There was an odd kind of poetry to it, Will would confide to her later, the strangled words indicating a whole ocean of feeling beneath. The dull green fields slid by the windows, a cow, a sheep, a tractor eliciting various responses. Their adult son would bunch the fingers of his bad hand together, and hammer his heart to indicate satisfaction, pleasure, maybe even love. The thoughts were complex, she could tell, although the words, the language even, were always simple, a capacity that was improving, the rehab centre had told her, day by day. But the silences were immense, and somehow, to all three of them, sweetness itself. And as Will drove up the avenue of elms and poplars towards the house, Alastair found the appropriate word, without any strain whatsoever.

"Home."

Could it really be home, she wondered, and could it really be that simple, as she unfolded the wheelchair by the portico and watched his father once more bear his weight so effortlessly and place him in the grey cushioned seat. She had to resist the urge to wheel him forward towards the door, but the wheels came to a stop at the lintel, and as Will worked the door key, Alastair allowed her to bend back the handles, crook the wheels forward and guide him inside.

And she watched Alastair now wheel his way past the grand piano and execute a rapid turn by the ivory keys. He reached his left hand out, which was his good hand, she now realized, and the ripple of notes that resulted gave her so much hope, for his future, and his recovery.

They were interrupted by a loud squawk from inside.

"A parrot," she told him, when his head made a surprised turn.

"Parrot," he repeated.

And the parrot, from inside the kitchen, began to whistle.

She watched her damaged son purse his lips and begin to whistle in turn.

"You know the tune?" she asked, barely daring to hope.

He nodded, and said with some difficulty:

"Satie."

"Erik," she said.

And she watched his good left hand move over the keys, playing a serviceable version of *Gnossienne No. 1*.

"Erik Satie," he said.

"Yes," she told him. "And that's the parrot's name, too."

And of course it wasn't that simple. It never could have been. And those simple words, love, one clenched fist pressed to the left-hand side of his chest, home, two interlocked hands making a rocking motion, were joined by others, as the rehab routine led to improvements in his speech, his sentence structure, his articulation of his thoughts, and with it, his past.

Two tortured fists, clenched together and viciously pulled apart, presaged his version of a three-syllable word which he one day managed. Abandoned. How could she? How could she have? How could she not have devoted the same care to him as she did to her beloved parrot?

She tried to explain. The times. Her situation. That basement flat in Brighton. She didn't mention her partner with the heroin habit, for fear of muddying his attachment to his father, Will. And she found it odd that none of the inarticulate blame fell on Will's shoulders. She talked with the rehab people, who told her in time her Alastair would manage another three-syllable word. Forgiveness.

They had prepared a room for him at the back of the rectory, overlooking the garden which he would one day tend with obsessive regard. That tendency towards obsession, the rehab therapist had told them, was one of the hallmarks of addiction. They should expect it to continue, as his physical condition improved. And his physical condition would improve, along with his articulation, with the correct motor skill and cognitive therapy, to which Will now devoted himself with all of the relentless enthusiasm of a new father in late middle age.

There was a therapeutic word for it, of course. Bonding. Was there a word for everything in this new world of theirs, Tara wondered, as she observed the father lift the son from the wheelchair to the downstairs bathroom as if he was an overgrown infant, which for the first six months could well have been the truth. He would clean him without complaint in the copper bath. And as Alastair's strength grew, they began a mutual exploration of the mysteries of horticulture. Will arranged a passage of planks around the grass, so Alastair could wheel himself amongst the bougainvillea, the winter-flowering cherry and magnolia and another small array of boards on upturned buckets and bricks which held his potted plants.

It was odd for her to watch an adult move through all the stages of childhood and another adult delight in the arrival of each momentous event. He made a better hand at fatherhood, she had to admit, than she had done at motherhood, even if his entire experience of it was this strange version, like a tune for the violin played on a double bass.

Alastair's right leg improved quicker than his right arm. That would always give him trouble, they were told, the dead arm that had the needle hanging from it. But with his left he could pick out the Satie, whistling as the parrot whistled in reply from the kitchen. And one day Tara came in from cycling and saw her

Alastair sitting on the piano stool, the wheelchair, like a baby's outgrown walker, beside it.

"You don't need it?" she asked and the reply came from Will, who was washing dishes in the kitchen.

"You have to see him walk."

"You can walk?" she asked her son.

"I can try," he replied and he placed both hands, with loud, discordant clangs, on the piano keys, and stood, moved awkwardly round the stool and gripped the handles of his wheelchair. He moved across the room towards his surprised mother and she held her arms out to embrace this fully grown child of hers.

But he didn't reach them. He kept going, past her outstretched fingers, into the arms of his father, Will, who had emerged from the kitchen, her own apron hanging untidily from his neck.

"Don't cry," Will said, as the tears flooded down her cheeks.

But the tears kept coming. And she found it hard to work out, were the tears for the arrival or departure of her only child?

47

A more amenable walker was given to them by the rehab, which was eventually replaced by two orthopaedic crutches and his gardening could then begin in earnest. She was allowed to join him in his horticultural endeavours. Which led to his attempt to clear the bed of nettles round the orchard and his discovery of a rancid sleeping bag amongst them.

"What is it?" he asked her and she wondered how she could have missed it.

Because of the nettles, of course.

Why there, she wondered, did his false predecessor sleep amongst the nettles like a tramp or one of those ancient Irish monks? "And then he returned, to his bed of nettles." It could have come from one of those hagiographies she had never really got round to reading. She came behind Alastair and grabbed a pitchfork and reached through the blistering heads of nettle and managed to spear the brown, ersatz cotton material and dragged it towards herself.

It was weighed down with something, and she didn't want him to find out what. It slipped from the grip of the fork, so she had to forage again, amongst the nettle roots this time. She dug the fork into the dark brown mouth of the bag, smelling, she had no doubt, of the dead one's nether regions, and managed to twist the prongs, tangle the material and drag it through the nettles towards her.

There was something buried inside it. So heavy that when her fork got a purchase on it, it cleaved a path amongst the nettle roots, like a giant, disembodied boot. What was all that weight, she wondered, and had a horrible image of severed heads, which she tried to dispel with a strange mad fancy of treasure, some kind of treasure, ancient coins, gold or plunder he had kept hidden. She dragged it to Alastair's feet, which, like the sleeping bag, were rarely bereft of surprises. She had a shiver of fear then, when the odour of the sleeping bag stung her nostrils. What if it wasn't treasure, but an animal corpse, a dog of his that had died and for some reason been kept hidden, or even worse, a human. Or even worse, a dead halibut, shark or conger eel that had been trapped on his nightline. So she untangled the fork from the mouth of the sleeping bag and speared the other end. She raised the fork, and the bag, straining with the effort of lifting whatever was inside. She could hear a rattle, more like a scrape, of a million tiny crab claws. And then they tumbled out.

Shells. Seashells. Scallop, clam, barnacle, razor, periwinkle and others the names she could not be bothered to remember. But she remembered coming out of the water in her distressed bathing suit to find him on the shore, collecting. Shells, he had told her, for the grotto.

"For the well," she said dumbly.

"What well?" he asked.

So she showed him. What remained of the trellis, the rectangle of rusting iron above the hole in the ground.

"There's a well underneath," she said, "with moss on the ancient walls. It falls into the earth and somehow it led me to you."

"How?" he asked.

She couldn't explain and hoped she would never have to. So she spoke about the rancid shells instead.

"I collected them from the seashore," she lied. "For a grotto."

Then another obsession began. The well, beneath its carapace of metal, the grotto, the healing powers of the water beneath.

"The moss," she told him.

"Moss," he repeated.

She discussed it with Will. The dead man's seashells, decorating a grotto.

"Sounds grotesque," she said.

"Grottesca," he said.

"What does that mean?"

"Cavern. Grotto."

They needed help with the cement mixer. Alastair's hands were too unsteady and a pianist's hands aren't designed for bricklaying. So Peter was press-ganged into brick and cement duties. He winched up the metal plate to uncover the well beneath. He designed a kind of igloo of bricks, and explained to Alastair how the brick at the apex kept the whole structure intact, magically held up by the urge to collapse into the darkness below. They both trowelled it then in concrete and the business of decoration began. Around the curved entrance first, which Alastair decorated obsessively with his unknown predecessor's shells. And when they ran out, she and her son foraged for more. Peter splayed the wet cement beyond the entrance, around the humped shoulders of the grotto, and each wet space was given its pressed seashell. It became a matter of pride, to have gathered them, found a vacant space amongst the brown cement, and pressed the maximum number of shells in. And while the orientally humped shape of the grey concrete grotto had first offended her, as its carapace of shells grew, she began to warm to it. Then the autumn rains came, adorning it with rust-coloured streaks, which softened it more. She awoke one morning to find a forest of ribbons tied to the hawthorn tree. The rumours were spreading again, and someone had visited, in the night or at dawn. Next she found cheap medals, miraculous ones, she remembered from her childhood, hammered into the cement of the grotto with tiny nails, to whatever surface of concrete remained exposed by the seashells. Always at night, or at dawn, or some other unseen hour. It was like an invisible cult beginning again, she told Will, a religion that didn't dare declare itself. Should we put up no trespassing signs?

But no, he shook his head. The well had done them too many favours. Until she was awoken the next morning by the sound of chanting and the smell of incense. She could hear it in the kitchen, a ghostly murmur which seemed to bounce around from floorboard to window and back again. She walked outside following the sound through the crab apple orchard to the well and grotto where a group in orange-coloured robes swayed gently, with burning clumps of wattle in their hands.

They were from the Tibetan meditation centre on the opposite peninsula. Profoundly apologetic, but they told her, in no uncertain terms, that the secret of the well could not be kept forever. It was out, and it was everybody's. All they needed for their website was the saint's name.

"They want a name," she told Will, hoping Alastair wasn't listening from the kitchen. Which of course he was.

"Ite," Will replied. "The beauty with the birthmark."

"Who lost it and found it again, every time she fell in the water. You must know by now that I made it all up."

Will raised a finger to his lips to hush her. But it was already too late.

"You made what up?" came her son's voice from the deal table.

"Your father found a well. It needed a story. And the story needed a saint. So I made it up."

"Why?"

"To punish him," she said. "But the punishment became something else. And led us both to you."

She walked into the kitchen and put her arms around his thin shoulders.

"You were nobody back then. And now you're somebody. So there's a well, but no saint. Or if there is, call him Saint Nobody."

But there already was a Saint Nobody, as he found, when he delved into that well of everything, the internet. Saint Nemo, which was, apparently, Latin for Nobody. As in Revelations 3:7: God closes and Nobody opens; Job 12:14: If God Imprisons a man it is Nobody who can release him.

"You're taking the piss," she said.

But he had already chosen a log from the woodpile and began to carve, or release, a name.

Nobody.

It was a pseudo-hagiographical text, William told her, from the middle ages. So maybe it was them, like her, taking, as she so elegantly phrased it, the piss.

She watched her son work with a penknife. Deft, assertive gouges. Woodcarving was one of the few talents he could cultivate from his wheelchair-bound days. His fingers had the scars to prove it. And after a while, she could distinguish the indented, faux-Germanic lettering:

Saint Nobody.

So they gave in. They allowed Alastair to erect the sign, hammered into the hawthorn tree. Saint Nobody's Well. Another, on the roadside, with a hand-drawn arrow. They allowed him to arrange his redundant orthopaedic devices around the grotto. The wheelchair, the walker, eventually even the crutches. As the rains came down, the rust on them grew, and they were joined, always unobserved and invisibly, by others. Old briar walking sticks at first, then cane and metal ones, strange three-legged walking devices which, amazingly, seemed to gather ancient rust as soon as they appeared. Peter playing tricks on us, she murmured to Will, but he replied that he couldn't be sure. She questioned Peter about it in the pub, paying him his final tranche for his work on the grotto, but he professed to know nothing about it.

"Maybe it's the saint," he said, returning to his pint. "What was that name again?"

"Nobody," she said.

She was amazed at the ease with which Saint Ite was forgotten, and Saint Nobody took her place. And she gradually got used to the sight, through the kitchen windows, of figures flitting through the undergrowth. She was unwilling to intrude on them, assumed whatever new-age practice they were following was none of her or Will's business.

Until one morning she found a gardening glove, lying in the bucket below the winch, above the rope that led to the well waters, far, far below. A left-hand glove, she realized, and was about to lift it out and return it to her son, when she saw it was stuffed, like a scarecrow's hand, with something that wasn't straw. She probed a finger into the glove's wrist and found herself touching moss. Moss from the ancient walls below. Dried moss, some of which tumbled out and fell in small bursts of licheny dust onto the rusting orb of the base of the bucket.

She heard music then, coming from the rectory, and dropped the glove, made her way through the boarded walks of Alastair's garden to the scullery door. She recognized the piece, and remembered it from many years ago in the Wigmore Hall. Ravel's *Concerto for the Left Hand*. She wondered should she make Will a cup of his favourite herbal tea as he practised, when she was surprised by the sight of him, entering from the living room. The piano kept playing.

"A record?" she asked. And then she realized the orchestra was missing.

"No," he whispered, and opened the door so she could see.

Alastair, left hand caressing the keys while his stiff right hand reached up to turn the sheet music.

"Commissioned," Will Barrow whispered, "by Paul Wittgenstein, brother of the philosopher Ludwig, who had lost his right arm in the First World War. The triumph of music over physical disability."

"I know," she told him.

"I remember."

Author's Note

I've taken inspiration from two movies for this novel. One is *Letter from an Unknown Woman*, by the great Max Ophüls (based on the book by Stefan Zweig), where a series of encounters are never remembered by the central character, a pianist. The other is *Lost Sex*, by the equally great but lesser known Kaneto Shindo, where a cleaning lady invents a legend to enable a relationship with a kabuki actor. I saw the first on late-night TV and have never forgotten it. I saw the second in the Astor on Burgh Quay, Dublin and never managed to forget it either.

About the Author

NEIL JORDAN is an Irish film director, screenwriter and author based in Dublin. His first book, *Night in Tunisia*, won a Somerset Maugham Award and the *Guardian* Fiction Prize in 1979. He is also a former winner of the Rooney Prize for Irish Literature, the Irish PEN Award and the Kerry Group Irish Fiction Award. Jordan's films include the Academy Award-winning *The Crying Game*, for which he won Best Screenplay, *Angel*, *Michael Collins* and *The Butcher Boy*.

Acknowledgements

Thanks to Neil Belton, Tamsin Shelton and
Aelred Doyle for their invaluable editorial input.
Thanks as well to John, the first reader.